A SIMPLE KISS

THE AMISH BONNET SISTERS BOOK 3

SAMANTHA PRICE

COPYRIGHT

CHAPTER 1

*P*ulling her woolen shawl snug around her shoulders to ward off the late afternoon breeze, Florence Baker made her way along the rows of apple trees in her orchard. It was wintertime, chilly but not bitter-cold today, and the trees' naked branches twisting toward the sky made a pleasant and artful sight.

No matter the season, she always found the trees beautiful. In the springtime, the trees woke from their winter slumber and sprouted the delicate, luminescent green leaves of new life. Then came the breathtaking show of white flowers that filled the air with sweet fragrance quite unlike any other. Spring was Florence's favorite season, but when blossoming season came to an end and the petals fell, they spread along the ground like a glorious blanket. As a child she had rolled around among the petals with one or both of her older brothers, and, even now as an adult she was often tempted to throw restraint to the wind and do the same.

It was pleasing to walk through the orchard every day and see so many changes take place.

Just witnessing so much beauty and grace filled Florence's heart to overflowing. Her daily walk was her escape from the struggles of life with six younger half-sisters and a stepmother who was weak—often in body and, more often, in mind. *Mamm* had never been the same since *Dat's* death two-plus years earlier. Neither had Florence, but someone had to run the household and the orchard. It had all fallen to her when her two brothers left shortly after the funeral. Even though the orchard was hard work, Florence couldn't imagine life without her trees. The orchard was her one connection to *Dat* and the times the two of them had walked here just as she did today, talking together about the trees and anything else that came to mind.

Today, Florence was finding it hard to let go of her troubles and soak in the beauty of the trees.

Every time she thought about Ezekiel Troyer coming to dinner tomorrow night, her stomach churned. Tomorrow evening was set to be memorable; she just knew it. Her stepmother and "Aunt" Ada had arranged Ezekiel's visit without her knowledge. They'd called it a surprise, but Florence considered the whole plot more of a shock. Especially when she found out Ezekiel was a pig farmer. That conjured up all kinds of images. There was no use protesting because—she soon learned—he'd already made plans to visit her community for a week. Who knew what *Mamm's* best friend, Ada, would've told him about her?

Would Ezekiel interest her more than her mysterious neighbor did? She hadn't seen Carter Braithwaite since he'd left her a gift of a grafted apple tree on her doorstep on Christmas morning. The note had said 'from a secret admirer,' but it had to have been from him. No one else knew she harbored the intention of looking for heritage varieties one day. She'd mentioned that very variety, and her intention of looking for it one day, only to him.

Since she'd received the gift, it'd played through her mind whether she should thank him or not... *But, if he wanted to be thanked, surely he would've used his own name—wouldn't he?* And if she did thank him, that would be clear and certain acknowledgment that he'd called himself an 'admirer' and was therefore fond of her.

She looked over at the setting sun, now a misty hazy ball glowing through the band of thin clouds at the horizon. It would be perfect and romantic—if only ... he wasn't an *Englischer,* and also if he wasn't slightly annoying at times.

Still, everything she repeatedly told herself about him being off-limits didn't stop her legs from taking her close to his property on each and every late afternoon stroll.

For the whole week, she'd stopped short of the fence line and lurked among the trees hoping to catch a glimpse of him to see what he was doing. His car was parked outside his cottage, but she'd not seen him. In the past, he'd come out of his house when he saw her nearby. Maybe if she stepped away from the trees ...

Why put myself in temptation's way? It will never be. She

grunted, wondering why she felt such a pull toward him if nothing would come of anything.

She smiled to herself when she heard Joy's voice in her head saying it must be *Gott* testing her. Joy, her third oldest half-sister, thought she had the answer to everything. Joy's comments on most things said that they were either *Gott's* blessing or *Gott's* testing. Florence stopped at a tree that she'd stopped at many a time before. It was far enough away that she wouldn't be seen from Carter's place.

Florence had often been judgmental of those who'd left the community for love, considering they had some weakness or were lacking in faith. Now she could see how hard it must've been for them. Perhaps *Gott* was prompting her to soften her heart and not be so 'judgy.' She'd never leave the Amish or her family, so thinking too much about Carter Braithwaite was a complete waste of time and energy. There was no chance of him joining her community. She knew that was so by a few of the off-the-cuff comments that he'd made. Besides that, she wouldn't feel safe or secure with a man who joined the Amish community for love.

When she saw a car drive slowly up the driveway toward his cottage, she lowered herself even further.

He never gets visitors.

He'd said he had no family, and had even referred to the cows he'd inherited from the previous owner as his friends. He'd been alone over Christmas, so who would be visiting him now? Every conversation she'd ever had with Carter zipped through her mind before the car came to a halt. She decided it was someone coming to give him a quote for renovations. He'd upgraded the kitchen and bathroom, and he'd been talking about redoing the rest of the place.

CARTER OPENED THE DOOR AND STEPPED ONTO THE PORCH, and Florence's heart rate accelerated. Her heart pumped so hard she could feel it pulsating inside her head. Breathlessly, she looked on as Carter hurried to the car while pulling down the sleeves of his black pullover sweater. When he opened the driver's door, a dark-haired woman got out and they exchanged a quick embrace.

The woman's slim frame was hugged by a pencil-thin skirt that ended just above her knees, and that was complemented by a fitted jacket of the same fabric. Her hair, bluntly cut, stopped precisely at her shoulders, and even from her hiding spot Florence could see the generously-applied makeup defining the woman's eyes.

The two spoke a few words before they walked toward the house. It was then that Florence saw the high heels and tinted sheer stockings. Carter had to be attracted to a woman like that. For the first time in her life, Florence felt an emotion she'd never experienced—jealousy.

This woman was no stranger; the embrace had said that much. They had to know each other. Even though there had been no passionate kiss, and no other affection had been shown apart from that embrace, the appearance of the stranger bothered Florence immensely.

Why is she there?

She kept watching until the woman walked inside ahead of Carter. He turned toward the orchard and Florence ducked back, even further out of sight. After a moment, she looked up to see both of them gone and the front door closing.

In her heart, the closing of the door was symbolic. He was on one side and she on the other. A wide, deep chasm existed between them, and the possibility of anything happening between herself and Carter was ... well, impossible.

It felt so bad.

Florence huffed and lowered herself to the ground. She pressed her back into the tree trunk. She desperately did not want Carter to like that woman. Even though she— being an Amish woman—couldn't marry him, she didn't want anyone else to have him.

As she nervously looped the hem of her apron back and forth between her fingers, she tried to talk herself out of liking him. He was a good-looking man, but it was hard not to be attracted to his personality too. He was funny and kind. Kind enough to have driven her around locally, looking for her runaway sister. Compassionate enough that he'd next driven her through the night and all the way to Connecticut to find the escapee, and then turning right around for the drive to bring them back home. Sweet enough to find her that rare apple tree. That must've taken him a long time. She couldn't imagine where he'd found it.

She groaned. Even though he referred to her half-sisters and herself as the "Bonnet Sisters," she felt she could overlook that one annoyance. It didn't seem so big in comparison to all his positive points.

Then she reminded herself she knew nothing about the man. He was a closed book, and there were so many things about him she ached to know. The biggest thing was, how did he get his money since he didn't appear to have a job? The couple of times she'd visited him, he'd been on his computer playing chess. As far as she knew, he couldn't make money from that.

Forget about him, she told herself. *That's the only thing to do.*

When other questions about Carter flew through her head, she fended them off with the speed of one of their barn cats chasing after a mouse.

There was no point wasting her thinking-time on Carter. He'd shown some interest in her as a person, but he'd asked no questions about her faith. If he was seriously interested in a close relationship, then surely, he'd want to know about her beliefs.

She pushed herself to her feet, turned, and rather than finish her walk, she headed home dragging her feet. It was possible Ezekiel Troyer could be her dream come true, and cause her to stop thinking about Carter.

When she was nearly at the house, she saw her stepmother walking toward her wiping her eyes. Florence wasn't used to seeing her stepmother teary-eyed. She normally floated over the top of life's problems. Florence bunched up the sides of her long dress in her hands and rushed toward her. *"Mamm,* what's wrong?"

"It's just that I'm upset over everything that's happened and I didn't want the girls to see me like this."

Florence put her arm around her and pulled her close. Wilma was just the right height to rest her head on Florence's shoulder. "What is it exactly that's upsetting you?"

"I feel like I'm losing control."

Florence didn't want to share with *Mamm* that the woman had never really had any control since *Dat* died. Florence had been required to step up and become the disciplinarian and leader of the household. "With what?"

"The girls. Look at what Honor did running away like that, and Cherish …"

"Both Honor and Jonathon apologized. Cherish is safely tucked away with Aunt Dagmar until she learns some sense, and Mercy is happily married. What exactly has upset you?"

Mamm sniffed and stood up straight, taking her head off

Florence's shoulder. "When you say it like that it makes me feel better. But ... things would be nicer if Mercy was still here."

"She's a grown and married woman, *Mamm,* and anyway, they said they'd be coming back to live here after a while."

"I know. I just hope that Honor and Jonathon don't try to run away again."

Slowly, Florence shook her head. "I don't think they will. Not now that you've given your approval of them being together." Another thing Florence didn't approve of, but *Mamm* because she was the mother, had gotten the final say.

"You don't like him, do you?"

Florence swallowed hard—she wasn't going to be so quick to forget what he had done, running away with Honor like that and putting everyone through such a great deal of stress. "I'm not the one who wants to marry him." Florence giggled making a joke out of it.

Mamm smiled. "That's true enough."

Then Florence realized she didn't want to make light of it, so she added, "I don't trust him. Well, I am trying, but ... let's just say I'm being cautious. You've told them they can't marry for a year. That should be long enough for us and her to see how he behaves."

"You're right as always."

"Is there anything else bothering you, *Mamm?*"

"I just hope Cherish forgives us for sending her away."

"It might take time, but I think we might've saved her from making a few big mistakes. Mistakes that might've ruined her life. She'll see that when she gets older."

"Do you think so?"

"I do. I know it. Now come on. Let's go back into the *haus*."

"I always wonder how different things would be if your *vadder* were still alive."

Florence put her arm around her stepmother's shoulder. "Me too. Every single day."

Mamm put her arm around Florence's waist and together they walked back to the *haus*.

CHAPTER 2

The next evening, Florence was mentally preparing herself to meet Ezekiel Troyer as she cooked the dinner alongside her stepmother and Hope, her fourth oldest half-sister. They were unusually silent as each went about preparing her part for their simple dinner of roasted meats and vegetables.

"I've lost count of how many are coming tonight," *Mamm* said.

"Me too," Hope said. "I'll count them up before I set the table."

They'd found out that morning that Joy had invited Isaac, her special friend, without checking if it was okay. The two of them had become inseparable over the last few days. When Honor learned Isaac was coming, she'd insisted Jonathon be there too.

Jonathon had apologized profusely to *Mamm* and Florence for running away with Honor. He'd also made amends with Mark and Christina for leaving his job at their store with no prior notice. Now he was back living in their stable quarters, but the job he'd so irresponsibly abandoned had been given to Christina's *bruder,* Isaac, the same Isaac with whom Joy had become friends.

JOY LEFT ISAAC IN THE LIVING ROOM AND HEADED TO THE kitchen. She poked her head around the door. "Need any help?"

Mamm turned around from stirring applesauce on the stove. "We'll be fine. Go back and talk with Isaac."

Joy noticed Florence didn't look too happy about that but she didn't say anything. Joy took one step toward the door and then turned back. "Did I tell you I invited Christina and Mark?"

"Nee! You didn't, did you?" *Mamm* asked.

"It's alright, isn't it? I thought I had to ask them to come because Isaac and Jonathon are coming." Joy shrugged her shoulders. "They would've been upset if we'd had a special dinner without them."

"It's not a special dinner." Florence's vivid blue eyes flashed with annoyance. "We just have a visitor coming along with Ada and Samuel. That's all."

"Have I done the wrong thing again? I always try to do the right thing and then people don't like it. I don't like leaving people out of something. How would you like to be left out of something, Florence?"

Florence pressed her lips together, and then through almost gritted teeth responded, "It's not like that. Fine, they can come."

"That's good because they're on their way already. It's too late to un-invite them."

"There's plenty of food," *Mamm* told Florence.

"I know. It's just that I didn't want a crowd of people watching me when I first meet Ezekiel. It'll make me nervous."

Joy said, "They won't do that. They're smarter than that." After Florence nodded and went back to grating dark chocolate over the mint frosting that covered the chocolate cake, Joy walked back out to Isaac. She was pleased to see him bending over and stoking the fire.

He glanced at her as she sat down. "They don't need any help?" he asked.

"They said not."

He placed the poker down, dusted off his hands and sat down beside her. He stretched his arms over his head and then rested one arm on the top of the couch behind her. "I have some news to tell you."

"What is it?"

"Jonathon has agreed to move out with me."

"Really?"

He nodded. "Well, it's not official yet. We can't do it unless he finds a job this week. I found a cottage for us to lease and it's so cheap it won't last long."

"Oh, good. Is it close by?"

"Not far from Mark and Christina's. Just a little further away than their *haus.*"

"I hope he finds a job soon, then. How's he doing with his job searching?"

"He reckons he's got a few possibilities."

She smiled and nodded, but that didn't mean anything to her. From what the family knew of Jonathon so far, he was a big storyteller and that was concerning. *Mamm* had managed to forget how Honor and Jonathon had run away. She'd swept it under the rug, but Joy could tell Florence wasn't so sure they wouldn't do something like that again. "Do you think you should move out with him?"

"Sure. It'll mean you and I can see more of each other."

Joy knew she had to choose her words carefully. "I know, and that's good, ...but, do you think Jonathon is the kind of person who should become a close friend of yours?"

"He already is. We get along great and he's a fun person to be around. We laugh all the time."

She looked down at the subtle swirling patterns on the dark rug beneath the couch and coffee table, wondering if

14

she should consider it an issue that Isaac thought Jonathon was suitable as a friend. She'd be happier if he found a friend who was more serious and Godly.

"What's wrong?" he asked.

She looked at him and saw genuine concern in his face. She had to be open and honest with him and not sugar-coat things the way most of her family members did. "It's just that I can't stop thinking about how he ran away with Honor. He's done some things that are not so good. And … you know what the Bible says about surrounding yourself with the righteous, don't you?"

The corner of his lips twitched as though he'd tasted something foul. "I thought everybody had forgiven him and moved past that."

"I know, but that's not what I'm talking about."

He breathed out heavily. "You're always saying what the Bible says, and doesn't *Gott* tell us to forgive? Even if we have to forgive someone over and over?"

She was pleased to hear him referring to the Bible. "That's true, but it also tells us that we need to choose our friends wisely. *He that walketh with the wise shall be wise: but a companion of fools shall be destroyed.* Are you doing that, Isaac?" She folded her arms across her chest. Didn't he want to be wise?

He withdrew his arm from behind her and stared at her open-mouthed. Then he slowly rubbed his jaw.

It was then she remembered someone had told her that men didn't like being told what to do. "Have I offended you?"

"You haven't, quite, but it sounds like you don't trust my judgement. Jonathon is fine and besides, it took two to run away. Why is it that the man always gets the blame? Your *schweschder* also ran away. Are you going to disown her—cast her out of your *haus?*"

"In this instance, it's because the man is so much older and should've known better. She's barely seventeen—not even legally 'of age' don't forget—and he's older than twenty."

Slowly, he nodded. "I guess that's true, but he told me he apologized and your mother accepted his apology."

She nodded. He was never going to agree. In a way, they were both right. She could see his point, just a little. "Let's talk about something else. How has it been, back living with your *schweschder* and *bruder*-in-law?"

When he chuckled, all the tension between them dissolved. "After living in the stable quarters for a few days, I kind of got used to being by myself and I'd like to do that again. It was hard to move back into the *haus,* but I figured that Christina would've been more comfortable with me moving back rather than—"

"Why couldn't Jonathon have moved in with his Aunt Ada and *Onkel* Samuel? They've got a big place."

"I guess he feels more comfortable around Mark. They do get along well together."

That made Jonathon letting Mark down even worse, in her estimation. Jonathon had suddenly left his job at the saddler store leaving Mark there by himself, but Joy considered it wise to leave that subject alone. "Why can't you get a place by yourself? Why do you need to move out with anyone at all?"

"I need someone to share the expenses. It'll be different living with a friend. He was ready to move out when he had a job, and now everything's reversed—I've got a job and he hasn't."

Joy giggled. "*Jah,* you got his job."

"That's right, and I'm keeping it!" He laughed. "I feel more than ready to live on my own now. When I say, 'live on my own,' I mean with someone my age but away from my *schweschder.* I can't wait to get out."

"If it's more money you need just ask Mark for a raise."

Isaac moved uncomfortably in his seat. "It doesn't work like that. He's only got a small business, remember, and I'm blessed to have a job there. There are plenty of people who'd love to have that job and would probably even work for less than he's giving me." He shook his head. "It's totally out of the question."

"Surely there's someone else you could move out with? Maybe someone who already has a job?"

"I don't know anyone else." He was quiet for a moment, and she could see something was bothering him. "Joy, why don't you trust my judgement? Jonathon is a perfectly fine and decent man. He made a couple of mistakes, but haven't we all? Your *Mamm* allowed your older sister to marry his *bruder,* Stephen, so doesn't that say something about the family he came from?"

"It says something about Stephen, but it doesn't necessarily say anything about Jonathon. The two of them are way different. Anyway, I'm sure Florence feels the same as I do even if *Mamm* doesn't."

They stared at one another for a moment, and then Isaac said, "Who's this 'special guest' who's coming to dinner? You haven't told me."

Joy knew he was trying to change the subject and she didn't mind. They'd never agree about Jonathon. She'd forgiven Jonathon already, since he'd apologized formally to *Mamm* and Florence, but that didn't mean she wanted the man she saw as a potential husband to be best friends with him. It was a recipe for disaster. "Just someone Ada and Samuel know. He's staying with them for a week or so."

When they heard a buggy, Joy was pleased for the interruption and jumped to her feet, hurried over, and looked out the window. "It's Honor and Favor home from the markets. I hope they had a good day. But not too good because I'll have to better it tomorrow." She giggled and spun around to face him while her long dress swished about her knees.

"Do you have competitions between yourselves?"

She sat back down next to him. "Not really, but I always like to have a good day of sales when I'm serving on the stall."

"I can understand that. I feel like that when Mark leaves the store for half a day. I try hard to make good sales— otherwise he'd maybe think I wasn't trying." He looked over toward the window. "Should I help them unhitch that buggy?"

"Nee, stay here and talk to me."

He chuckled. "Okay."

CHAPTER 3

*O*nce they were all sitting in the living room, Joy returned to the kitchen to see how close dinner was.

"Is everyone here already?" asked Florence, looking a little anxious.

"Nee," said Joy. "I was just wondering. We're still waiting on about half of the people; Ada and Samuel, Ezekiel, Mark and Christina, and Jonathon too." Joy noticed how worried Florence looked. Fine lines appeared on her forehead, and then she noticed Florence's soiled apron. It wouldn't make a good first impression for Ezekiel to see Florence like that. "Do you want me to take over while you get ready, Florence?"

Holding a wooden spoon in one hand, Florence looked down at her clothes. "I was going to change my apron, naturally." She looked back up at Joy. "Is this dress okay?"

"I think you should wear one of your better dresses, don't

21

you? This is just an everyday dress. It's a dress you'd wear to pin out the washing."

"Jah, you're right. I'll get changed now before the rest of them arrive."

"Jah, that's best."

Florence turned to *Mamm* and handed her the wooden spoon. "I won't be long. I was just about to make the gravy."

"Take your time. I'll do the gravy in a minute."

"And I'll help *Mamm* with that," Hope said, stepping forward.

"Denke." Florence felt good that all the girls were coming together to help. That was what family did when it was needed, but sometimes her sisters needed prompting.

Florence briefly greeted Isaac in the living room as she hurried past to walk up the stairs. She hoped the night wouldn't be too dreadful. Now she was grateful for all the extra people who'd been invited. With more people, there was less chance of awkward pauses in the conversation at the table.

She pushed open her door and then with both hands flung open the double wooden doors of her closet. Her sudden burst of strength popped a nail and dislodged the top hinge and now the right-hand door was hanging down. Florence sighed. Another job to add to her list of things for tomorrow. With no man in the household, it was Florence's job to do all the fiddly maintenance work, and the list for those tasks had become never-ending. She'd become well-acquainted with her father's old tools and had taught herself to use them.

She turned her attention back to her clothes, and reached for the green dress. *"Nee!"* she said aloud. That was her best and she didn't want to look like she was trying too hard. If it turned out she liked him, she could wear her best dress at the Sunday meeting.

After she pulled off the 'pinning out the washing dress,' she took hold of the grape-colored dress—her second-best—and decided on that one. She'd been told the color made her eyes "light up."

As she stepped into her dress, she was filled with dread over the night ahead. There wasn't much chance of this man being everything for which she'd hoped. For one thing, he lived in the wrong location, and she doubted he'd willingly leave his farm to move closer. Leaving her orchard wasn't an option either. She'd rather stay single forever than do that. Amongst her apples she was at peace, contented. Surrounded by her trees, she felt close to her parents and the life she'd briefly shared when they'd both been alive.

Once she'd dressed, fixed her hair and placed on her *kapp*, she sat down on her bed and closed her eyes.

Dear Gott, *I'm ready for you to find me someone who suits me.*

That was her prayer and although it was brief, it said

everything on her heart. Then she lay down on her bed thinking, as her head sank into her pillow.

The thinking soon turned into worrying, as it so often did. What if the man who suited her wasn't the one she wanted? God might think she needed trying and testing over things and the last thing she wanted was to face complications. She'd seen her best friend Liza struggle trying to make her marriage a happy one. Now, *Gott* had blessed her marriage with happiness, but Liza had been sad for years.

Florence would rather be tested in other ways. Being close to Liza and seeing what she'd been through was the main reason she'd cautioned her sisters into taking their time to make sure the men they married were just right for them.

It wasn't until Mercy got married that Florence thought about marriage as a reality for herself. Time had passed her by so quickly. The couple of men she'd liked in her younger days had not looked twice at her, neither one of them, and now they were married. After that, Florence had put love and marriage out of her mind.

Florence got up and moved to the window and stared out. In the distant semi-darkness, the lights of a buggy came into view. She watched as it came closer, and then she moved back so no one in the buggy would see her.

The first person out of the buggy was a man. Not Samuel, although it was Samuel and Ada's buggy. It had to be Ezekiel Troyer. He was tall, a little on the heavy side and from the distance she was to him, she wasn't repulsed at all like she'd expected. In fact, she was pleasantly surprised by the kindness of his face. Ada had done well. She'd chosen Stephen for Mercy and that had worked splendidly. Now, Florence only hoped Ezekiel's personality would be as pleasing as his looks.

Tying her *kapp* strings under her chin, she backed away and then hurried downstairs to be the first to meet him. By doing so, she'd feel less nervous.

When she reached the bottom of the stairs, her stepmother had her hand on the front door handle. She turned around and said to Florence, "Do you want to open the door?"

"You do it," Florence said, changing her mind on the spot.

Her mother flung open the front door before Florence could step aside, and the next thing she saw was Ezekiel smiling at her. Florence stepped forward and reached out her hand. "Hello. Ezekiel, is it?"

He took off his hat and offered his large hand for her to shake. It was delightfully warm. "That's me, and you must be Florence?" His accent was a little different from what she was used to. He spoke with slightly drawn-out words, almost sounding melodious.

Removing her hand from his, she said, "That's right. Florence Baker." To take the attention off herself, she introduced her stepmother and then Samuel and Ada joined them. Everyone else came out from the living room, eager to meet the visitor.

After all the introductions were done, Ezekiel said to Wilma, "How many girls do you have, Mrs. Baker?"

"Please, call me Wilma. I have six, but the oldest is married and has moved away. My youngest is staying with her aunt for a time." She lightly touched Florence's shoulder. "Seven *dochders* counting Florence. She's my step-*dochder.*"

Florence fixed a smile on her face. Why did *Mamm* always have to make that distinction? Why couldn't she just say she had seven daughters? Was it necessary to announce to all that Florence wasn't her biological daughter? Was she ashamed of her? It was something Wilma had always done and there hadn't been one time that it hadn't bothered Florence. It made her feel second-best.

"Can I help you in the kitchen, Wilma?" Ada asked.

"Nee. We're all done. Is everyone hungry?"

"I'm starving," Favor said, earning a glare from *Mamm.* "Well, I am."

Hope said, *"Mamm,* we're still waiting for Jonathon as well as Mark and Christina."

"Oh, that's right. They're not here yet," *Mamm* said looking around.

"Here they come now," Samuel said, looking out the still-open front door.

While they waited for the rest of the guests, Isaac and Joy talked to Ezekiel. Florence backed into the kitchen to start placing the food into the serving bowls. Whenever the family had many guests, it was always a help-yourself affair with the food placed down the center of their long table.

When the final guests arrived, another lot of introductions took place, and then Florence called everyone to their dining room, a room that was adjacent to their kitchen. With having no allocated seats for the guests, Florence was the one who suggested where everyone sat. Since *Mamm* and she were the ones doing the serving, they sat closest to the kitchen. When Florence was only halfway through her seating suggestions, Ada butted in and told Ezekiel to sit down right next to the chair where Florence was to sit. Florence had planned to put at least one person between them.

Once everyone was seated and their silent prayers of thanks for the food had been given, the bowls of food were passed around while everyone helped themselves.

Immediately, Florence noticed that Honor and Jonathon were talking exclusively to each other. It had been a mistake to seat them together.

"Did you have a good apple season this year? I mean, last year?" Ezekiel asked Florence, seeming to feel just as awkward as she felt.

"It was one of our best. We always try to do better than

the previous ones, but that is dependent upon the weather."

"And *Gott*," Joy butted in.

Florence looked over at Joy sitting to the other side of Ezekiel. She hadn't even realized Joy was listening. *"Jah. And Gott's* will," Florence agreed.

"That's something that normally goes unsaid," Ezekiel commented to Joy. "I'm sure Florence—"

"It shouldn't go unsaid. When we talk about *Gott* that brings Him into our presence, like He's sitting at the table with us. Matthew 18: 20 says, *where two or more of my people are gathered I am in their midst.*" Now everyone stopped their conversation and all eyes were on Joy. She lowered her head slightly. "That's what I think anyway."

Ezekiel said, "It's good to talk about Our Lord and Savior."

Florence smiled, pleased he was supporting Joy.

Isaac said, *"Jah,* and it's *gut* that we can all be free to have our say."

Favor snickered. "You don't know the half of that."

Everyone looked at Favor and Florence had no idea what she meant. Was it because Joy was constantly telling them all what the Bible said?

Suddenly Samuel's voice broke through the stunned

silence, the second in less than three minutes. "These potatoes are delicious."

"They're just normal everyday potatoes," *Mamm* said.

"I think they taste creamier than usual."

"Nee. They're just the same."

Ada joined in. "I think they're good too and I love this crispy-skinned chicken."

"I've already given you the recipe for that," *Mamm* told Ada.

"Jah, and you've given it to me too," Christina said. "But I must remember to make it sometime. I've been too busy with other things."

Florence was grateful that everyone was talking now, rather than Joy dominating. It made things tense having to watch what she said around Joy every day.

Ezekiel rested his knife and fork against his plate, "I see you've got a shop down by the road. When does that open?"

Mamm said, "We open that in the warmer months. It does especially well at harvest time."

"I see."

"That's why we have the market stall in the colder months," Honor said.

"You don't have it all year?"

Florence explained, "We have been at the markets all year, but this has been the first year to try it, so we're not sure if we'll keep going with that. It needs two people, and it's a lot of travel there and back every day."

"We'll see what happens," said *Mamm.*

Ezekiel turned to Florence's older brother, Mark. "And you don't work in the orchard?"

He shook his head. "*Nee.* I have a saddlery store. Isaac works for me," he said with a nod toward his *bruder*-in-law. "Isaac's Christina's *bruder.*"

"Ah, now I'm making some connections." Ezekiel nodded, and then looked at Jonathon. "Where do you fit in, Jonathon?"

Florence desperately wanted to say that he didn't fit in at all, but unfortunately Mercy was married to his brother. That made Jonathon Mercy's *bruder*-in-law, and therefore as good as family to all the rest of the Bakers.

"The oldest Baker sister is married to my younger brother."

"That's Mercy and Stephen," Hope told Ezekiel.

"Hmm. It'll take me a while to remember all this."

Favor rolled her eyes. "Don't even try. I can't even remember it."

"That's because you don't care about anyone other than yourself," Joy told her.

Mark took on the older brother role. "I'd hate for any of you girls to have to finish your meals in your rooms..."

Favor looked down. "Sorry, Mark."

"*Jah*, sorry," Joy mumbled.

"I'm sure Joy didn't mean anything bad," Isaac said.

A few chuckles were heard around the table and no one made any further comment.

WHILE THEY WERE WAITING AT THE TABLE FOR DESSERT, JOY leaned over and whispered to Isaac, "Thanks for helping me out before. No one understands me."

Isaac gave her a big smile. "Well, I do."

She looked at his flushed rosy cheeks and was glad. "*Jah*, you do, but no one else does."

"Will you be at the markets tomorrow?"

"*Jah*. I'll be there again tomorrow."

"If I get a chance, I'll come see you."

"That would be *wunderbaar*. I'd like that."

"I might get a half hour for lunch, but not if we're too busy."

"Okay. I'll keep an eye out for you."

Joy listened to Ezekiel and Florence over dinner. He was a plain man, pleasant mannered, and he looked like a good strong man—and that was perfect seeing as he was a farmer. From Florence's guarded expressions, Joy couldn't figure out what her half-sister thought about him. It wasn't ideal that he lived two hours away, but if they loved each other, things like that could be worked out.

CHAPTER 4

*W*hen dinner was over, everyone sat down in the living room while Joy and Honor made the after-dinner coffee.

Honor wrung her hands. "I hope Florence isn't going to be mean to Jonathon."

"Of course she won't."

"I know she doesn't like him—and he knows it too. She's still mad at us."

"She's trying to impress Ezekiel, so she wouldn't be mean to someone while she's trying to impress him."

Honor left off filling the kettle and peered around the doorway into the living room. Then she faced Joy. "Do you think Florence likes Ezekiel?"

"I do. He's perfect for her."

"I don't know if she'll ever marry anyone. I can't imagine her with him or anyone else."

"I think she'll take it slow."

Honor giggled. "Years even, from how she keeps telling us to slow things down."

"I think you're right."

Honor walked over to the sink and finished filling the kettle. "Sometimes I regret coming back here." She lit the stove and placed the kettle on the flame.

"Nee. You did the right thing. You would've had a dreadful life if you didn't come back. Jonathon mightn't have been able to find work and then you two would've been living as *Englishers* and might never have come back to the community—ever."

"I got the sweet taste of freedom when I was away. There're too many people looking over my shoulder." Honor grabbed the coffee container. "It's strangling me."

"It's called family. And people only keep an eye on you because they care about you."

"What's annoying about you, Joy, is that you have an answer for everything."

"And that annoys you?"

"Jah, it does." Honor shook the coffee into the plunger.

"Next time you ask me something, I'll say I don't know."

"Gut."

Joy got the mugs ready to place on the tray. "Have we got any of that chocolate cake left?"

"Jah, um, *nee.* That one's gone. Florence made a fresh chocolate cake with mint frosting for tonight, and Favor made cupcakes this morning and candies, too." They prepared trays with plates of either cake or cupcake, and forks and napkins. They added a dish of the candies to each tray so everyone could help themselves.

The two girls took a tray each of the coffee fixings out to the living room and then Honor kneeled to pour while Joy passed a cup of coffee to each person. They went back into the kitchen after that, and brought out the cakes and the candies.

FLORENCE AND EZEKIEL WERE SEATED NEXT TO ONE another again, and when all of the others were talking in groups, Ezekiel smiled at her and said, "Would you have some spare time to spend with me tomorrow?"

"Of course. What would you like to do?"

He wrapped his fingers further around the white coffee mug, resting it on his knee holding it only by his fingertips. "What kind of things are there to do around here?"

"That's a hard one to answer because most of the time I'm

here at home." She rarely went anywhere unless it was to go somewhere with Liza.

"When you go out, where do you go?"

"Mainly I visit people, go to the meetings, or go to the markets."

His face lit up. "Perfect—the markets. I wouldn't mind having a look around the markets." He took a mouthful of coffee.

"Really?"

He nodded. "Yes."

Jonathon called from across the room. "What caused you to visit us, Ezekiel?"

Everyone was silent and looked over at Ezekiel. Florence was embarrassed and wondered what he'd say. "It was Ada's fault," he joked. "She said I should visit them for a weekend and I've never been here, so I decided it was a good idea."

"Who's looking after your pigs."

Florence frowned at Jonathon. She could tell he was mocking Ezekiel.

"My two younger brothers."

"And what do you hope to do while you're here?"

Florence wanted to say something to silence the trouble-making Jonathon, but she couldn't think what. She saw one candy left on a plate and she was half inclined to toss it at him.

"Make new friends. And I had hoped to meet Florence, and now I have." Ezekiel looked over and smiled at Florence.

It was a good way to defuse Jonathon. He went quiet, apparently without a comeback, and then—to Florence's relief—went back to talking to Samuel.

AN HOUR LATER, FLORENCE WAS STANDING BESIDE *MAMM* waving goodbye to Samuel, Ada, and Ezekiel. Just before Ezekiel left, he made arrangements to collect Florence the very next morning.

When they walked back inside the house, Jonathon laughed loudly about something and that was the final blow that grated on Florence's nerves. Then and there she decided someone needed to talk with him about trying to embarrass Ezekiel. "Can I speak to you for a moment, Jonathon?"

He looked up at her, shocked. "Sure."

She nodded her head toward the door. "Outside."

He left his seat beside Honor and stepped out onto the porch with her. "What is it?" He looked sick with worry.

"I'm upset with you. Do you know why?"

He drew his eyebrows together and seemed confused. "No. Over what?"

She studied his face. There was no hint of amusement. "Well, you know Ezekiel came here to see me, don't you?"

He pulled a face. "No. No, I didn't know that. I'm sorry; now I feel like a fool. Honor never mentioned it. And I didn't think about it myself because I never thought you'd be interested in someone like him."

His comment jolted her. *Someone like him?* "Do you know anything about him?"

"No. I've never met him until today."

"What did you mean by your comment? You said, *'someone like him.'*"

Jonathon said. "I'm sorry. I shouldn't have said that." He shook his head. "I keep putting my foot in it, don't I?"

"That's okay. I can't blame you for speaking your mind."

"I'm sure you're not interested in what I think about him or anything else."

She had to smile about that. Why was she worried what Jonathon thought about Ezekiel? She wasn't sure whether she did care to hear his opinion, but she would've liked to know how other people viewed Ezekiel. "Don't worry about it. You go inside now and spend some time with Honor."

"Okay, and don't worry, he seems a swell guy."

"Denke, Jonathon, and I'm sorry to blame you for what you said to Ezekiel earlier. I thought you were trying to embarrass him, or me, or maybe both."

"I hope you know now that I wasn't. It seems Honor doesn't tell me everything."

"It's okay, I believe you."

"I'd better get back inside before Honor gets jealous." He gave her a cheeky wink before he slipped through the doorway.

Florence stared into the night sky for a moment. Had Jonathon just used his charms and talked his way out of trouble? She sighed in dismay at her iffy people-reading skills.

Not yet ready to return to the noisy house, she lingered in the crisp night air. Looking into the still night, she leaned against the porch railing thinking some more about Ezekiel.

He was nice.

She blew out a deep breath. It was far too soon to know if there was a future with him. They'd have to spend more time together to allow their relationship to bloom. And, like a carefully tended plant, perhaps love would grow between them.

It was times like these Florence missed the guidance of her mother. It wasn't something she could bring herself to discuss with Wilma.

CHAPTER 5

*I*t was nine o'clock Friday morning, the time that Ezekiel had arranged to collect Florence. She already felt like she'd done a day's worth of chores. Besides making breakfast for everyone, and organizing the cooking for the day, she'd hammered the nail back into her closet door, put the sliding door of the utility room back onto its track, and found some left-over paint in the shed to re-paint the back door of the house. The painting itself was a project for another day.

Having done enough work so she wouldn't feel guilty for the free-time she was taking today, she sat nervously next to *Mamm* in the living room hoping the day would go well. She was so anxious that she found it hard to sit still.

Honor and Joy had gone to the markets while Hope and Favor were in the kitchen starting the first lot of cooking —a batch of applesauce—before Hope headed to the store at the front of the family home at nine thirty. After that,

Favor and *Mamm* would cook the remainder of the items on Florence's list.

"You look so nervous," *Mamm* commented to Florence.

Florence swallowed hard. "Do I?"

Mamm nodded.

"I am, more than a little." Florence smoothed down her dress and then spread her apron out to cover it. *"Denke* for helping Ada arrange this."

"I didn't do anything at all. It was Ada who did everything. I didn't even know him. It's good that he wants to go to the markets because you'll be able to keep an eye on the girls."

Florence didn't want to worry about having to check on her sisters today of all days. "I'm sure they'll be okay, and if not I can't do anything about it. I just want to concentrate on Ezekiel and get to know him."

"And you should." *Mamm* patted her on the shoulder and then she glanced at the clock on the mantle. "Oh dear, it's two minutes after. I hope he's not one of these tardy people." *Mamm* disliked it when people were late.

"I don't think so. He doesn't know the area. He could've taken a wrong turn, or something could've gone wrong with the horse. Anything could've happened."

"Well, I suppose we'll soon find out. I do like him. I think he'll suit you fine. You have several things in common."

Florence screwed up her nose. "Like what?"

"His father has gone home to *Gott* leaving him to run his farm and so has yours."

"My *vadder?*"

"Jah. Yours has gone to be with *Gott* too."

"That's true, but we don't have a farm." Florence kept a straight face. She knew she was being difficult, but she couldn't help it.

"I'm sure running an orchard and a farm are very similar."

"I guess so."

"And he's helping his *mudder* just like you're helping me."

Florence was certain she had things tougher. "He's only got two younger brothers, and I've got all our girls to worry about. I wonder if he'd trade places?"

Mamm put her hand up to her mouth and giggled. "You've only got four to worry about now and next year you might only have three. But by then, you might be married to Ezekiel." Her stepmother's eyes twinkled.

Florence knew *Mamm* hadn't even considered any ramifications a marriage to Ezekiel would bring. What would become of the orchard if she moved away? "Let's not get ahead of ourselves. I want to make sure he's right for me."

"Of course, I wasn't suggesting anything else."

Florence leaned back in the couch and closed her eyes.
There was no reason he wouldn't be suited to her. He was
the right age, and he seemed even-tempered and polite.
On top of that, he was hard-working, a trait that was
important to Florence.

Favor flew out of the kitchen. "He's coming, he's coming!"

Florence bounded to her feet. "Shush. He'll hear you."

Amidst peals of laughter, Favor ran back into the
kitchen.

Florence exchanged anxious looks with Wilma. It seemed
a lot hinged on this day. Perhaps her entire future. While
Florence was in the middle of wrapping her shawl around
her shoulders, there was a loud knock on the door. *Mamm*
pushed past her to open it.

"Ezekiel, this is a nice surprise," Wilma said.

"Didn't you know I was coming? I arranged with Florence
last night to take her out for the day. I hope it hasn't
slipped her mind."

"Of course it hasn't. Come in."

Before he had a chance to move, Florence appeared from
behind the door. "Hello."

"Hello, Florence." He looked down at his feet. "Are you
ready? I don't want to come in because my feet are
muddied from all the rain we've had."

"I'm ready." She gave her stepmother a quick kiss on the

cheek before she accompanied him out of the house and down the porch stairs.

"Do you always get this much rain here?" he asked.

"No, not really." She stepped carefully avoiding the puddles. "We do need the rain, though."

Once they were in the buggy and traveling down the driveway, she hoped the conversation would flow easily. "I guess your brothers will be missing your help on the farm by now."

"They'll be fine as long as they work a bit harder. I'd like to get my mother a gift from the markets today. Do you think they'll have anything suitable there?"

"They should. They sell all kinds of things there, not just fruit and vegetables. I'll enjoy this. I haven't been shopping for some time. Looking at all the pretty things will be nice. What did you have in mind?"

She looked over at Carter's house as they rode past. There was no one about.

Ezekiel looked over at her. "I thought you might be able to give me some ideas."

She laughed. "Me?"

He nodded. "You're a woman, so you know what women like."

"I guess so, but that's a big responsibility. Tell me a bit about your mother."

"You remind me of her."

Florence stared at the road ahead. That wasn't what she wanted to hear. Did she look like an old person to him? His mother had to be at least fifty, and she was only in her mid-twenties.

She had to ask, "In what way do I remind you of her?"

"The way you're always making sure that others are okay."

Immediately, she was relieved. He didn't think she looked much older than her years like Mercy's husband had thought when he first met her. Stephen had presumed she was Mercy's mother, at first, rather than her half-sister. "You could tell that just from last night?"

"I'm a pretty good judge of people and I know what it's like to be the eldest. We are both the oldest in our families."

"I'm not the eldest. I have two older brothers. You met Mark last night, and then there's Earl. He's moved away to Ohio."

"But you're the oldest living at home, aren't you?"

"That's true. Well, I hope I'll be able to steer you in the right direction to find a suitable gift."

"I'm sure you will."

"It'll be a lot of pressure." She giggled.

"When I said you reminded me of my *mudder,* I didn't

mean you're as old as she is or anything." He chuckled. "I meant she's the nicest person I know."

"Oh, I'm glad to hear it. I was a little worried." She smiled at him.

"I wasn't talking about looks. For starters, she doesn't have your amazing blue eyes. She has the same boring brown eyes as I do."

"Brown eyes are lovely. They're not boring at all."

"I guess it's a matter of opinion. They serve me well to look out from. I'm pleased I don't have to look at them. I'd rather look at yours."

She couldn't help smiling at the corny compliments. She was reminded of the first time she met Carter. He too had commented on her eyes.

When Ezekiel kept smiling at her, she pushed Carter Braithwaite from her mind. Today was about getting to know Ezekiel Troyer and not to think about someone who was *verboten.*

"It's been awhile since I've been away from the farm, and I must say I'm enjoying it." He cast a sidelong look at her.

She nodded and did her best to stay focused on Ezekiel and him alone. "I can imagine how that would feel."

"When did you last take a vacation?"

"Hmm, let's see now." The last time she'd been away from the farm was when Carter Braithwaite drove her overnight to bring Honor home when she'd run away with Jonathon, but that probably didn't count. It certainly hadn't been any fun. "I can't remember. I think the last time was when *Dat* was still alive and we went visiting."

"And how long has it been?"

"Over two years now. Vacations aren't that important to me. I'd rather stay at home with my apple trees." He might as well find out early on that she was devoted to her orchard. That was how she'd been raised. She'd loved the orchard as much as her father had, which was just as well because her two older brothers hadn't been the least bit interested in taking it on after *Dat's* funeral.

"That's exactly what I used to say as well until I started taking little trips away. A couple of days here and a couple of days there. Now, a week here."

"Maybe one day I'll take a vacation."

"Perhaps you might come to my farm to visit me?"

She glanced at him again to see him smiling at her. "Maybe." She had to change the subject. It was too soon to commit to visiting him. "It's mostly food there."

"What's that?" Confusion wiped the smile from his face.

"At the farmers markets. Sorry. It's mostly food."

"I thought it was an arts and crafts market. Where I come from, the markets have food in one section, and the other section sells all kinds of wares."

"Nee, this one is mostly foods, some flower vendors, too, but I can take you to one of those if you want."

"Jah, please. Can we go there after the farmers market? I'd like to see your stall."

"Okay, but don't expect too much. Many others have built-in shelves and countertops. We only have trestle tables because we don't know for how long we'll keep the stall. We already have the shop at the front of the *haus,* so …"

"I'd like to take a look none the less."

"Sure. It's not very far from the other markets where you'll be able to find a gift."

"Okay, looks like we're having a market day."

Florence smiled. "It seems like it."

"Are you going to see how the market stall turns out? See if it's worthwhile?"

"That's exactly right. We're comparing it to the roadside stand we had up until recently—until the cold weather arrived. There's no rent for that, of course. But it's too cold in the winter for the girls to stand out there without shelter or heat."

"That's true about the rent, but there'd also be less traffic to bring customers."

"That's it, exactly. Years ago, when we were younger, my *vadder* put our fruit and vegetables on a table on the roadside with an honesty box. Turns out, people weren't that honest—a lot of them. So, when we got older, two of us were there all the time. We sold a lot more that way, and it stopped the losses, too. And just this winter, we decided to see how a market stall would do."

"Has it been worth it?"

"It has so far, but it's a lot of extra work and the extra traveling time, so we have to weigh it up." She shook her head. "With two of my sisters gone now, we're feeling the extra work."

"I understand. Our main method of sale for our pigs is through our local farmers market."

"Is that so?"

"That's right. *Mamm* runs it, along with a couple of girls she's hired from the community. Our pigs are grass fed and there's a lot of demand for that nowadays."

"That's good for you, then."

He chuckled. "Yes, it is. We do alright."

"It sounds like your *mudder* works hard with running the household and the stall."

"That's also how you remind me of her. From what I heard over dinner last night, you're just as busy."

"And that's the way I like it."

"Same with my mother, and she does charity work as well."

While Florence was smiling on the outside, she wasn't happy about being compared to his mother. "We do charity work as a family sometimes, too."

When they walked through the market stalls, he showed great interest in the meat section, and even stopped to ask the operators questions.

"Getting ideas?" she asked when he finished.

He chuckled. "They do have good displays. This market is a little nicer than ours." He chuckled. "Ours is a lot smaller besides." He looked along the row of stalls. "They just go on forever."

"I know. And our stall is right at the back. Follow me."

They strolled along one of the rows until they came to Honor and Joy. They were busy serving, so they just waved at them while Ezekiel had a quick look at the stall. Then they kept moving.

"I wonder if Ada needs anything. I should've asked before I came here."

"It's not likely. Ada and *Mamm* trade fruit and vegetables between themselves. What one wants, they just take from the other, and Samuel gets meat from his *bruder*."

"I didn't know Ada and your mother were so close."

"They've been best friends ever since I can remember."

"It seems that Ada is one of those people who knows everyone."

"She and Samuel travel to other communities a lot. Samuel doesn't work every day now that he's older and it gives them the time to do it."

After they walked up and down more of the aisles, Florence was getting a little bored, but Ezekiel seemed to be enjoying himself. "Are you ready to go to the other markets now?" she asked, giving him a gentle hint.

His attention was taken by something else. "Feel like a bite to eat first?"

She suddenly realized how hungry she was and followed his gaze to one of the two cafes at the entrance of the markets. "Okay. That'd be nice."

"Will this place be okay, or do you know somewhere else that's better?"

"I believe the food's nice here, although I've never tried it myself."

He sniffed the air. "The smell of the coffee is what got to me."

"Let's try it." They both walked into the cafe that was near the front of the markets. They sat down and he passed her one of the two menus on the table.

"Order anything you like, my treat."

"Denke." She scanned down the menu. "I think I might have a toasted cheese and bacon sandwich."

"Is that all?"

"That's all I feel like. And maybe a coffee. Since that's what pulled us into this place." She finished looking at the menu and looked across at him. "What will you have?"

"I think I'll have the spaghetti Bolognese."

"That sounds nice."

"Do you want to change your order?"

She shook her head. *"Nee."*

They stayed at the cafe for another hour, talking and eating, and ended up having a second cup of coffee.

They both finished their last swallow at the same time and then stared at one another, smiling.

"Are you ready to go?" he asked

"I am, but I'm still nervous about picking out a gift for your *mudder.*"

He laughed. "Also, Ada. I'll get something for her allowing me to stay at her place."

As Florence rose to her feet, she said, *"Ach!* Even more pressure."

Ezekiel laughed. "I'm sure you'll be okay. You'll do fine. And selecting something for Ada should be easier since you know her."

"I'll try my best."

CHAPTER 6

Soon after Joy had spotted Florence and Ezekiel as she looked up from her stall, Isaac appeared. Joy quickly turned around looking in all directions for Florence, but she'd gone.

Fortunately for Joy, the number of customers had lessened, so she left Honor by herself and went to speak with Isaac. He wore his usual grin.

"I don't have long," he told her.

"Neither do I, or Honor will complain."

"I just saw Florence and Ezekiel. They didn't see me. They were sitting down eating and looked pretty cozy."

"That's interesting. I saw them too about five or maybe ten minutes ago. I don't know what they were doing here. Probably keeping an eye on us. Florence would've been, anyway."

His face lit up with mischief. "She doesn't need to do that, does she?"

Joy shrugged. *"Nee,* but it's just strange for them to be here."

Isaac's eyes sparkled with humor. "They looked like they were getting along."

"Did they?"

"Jah, they look like an old married couple."

Joy giggled and shoved his arm slightly. "I'll tell her you said that."

He chuckled. "You'd better not. I don't want to end up on the wrong side of Florence like Jonathon is."

"Yeah, I know what you mean, but she's just trying to protect Honor."

"I know that's the reason, but still …"

"Let's not waste time talking about anyone else. I couldn't wait to see you today."

His grin got wider. "Me too."

"I was hoping and praying you would come to see me. How did you get the time off?"

"It's my lunch break."

"It's a little late for that, isn't it?"

"We were busy, so I waited to take my lunch when it got

quieter. Now, I have to hurry back."

Joy pouted. "Do you have to go already? You only just got here."

"I have to. I really should stay in the back room to eat. Normally I would, but I just had to come see you." He took her hand and squeezed it and her heart melted. "What time should I collect you tomorrow?"

"I'll be doing chores until twelve, so, any time after that."

"One minute after twelve." He raised his eyebrows and she giggled again.

"That's fine by me. Wait!" She shook her head. "I'm working here again tomorrow."

"But it's my day off and we planned—"

"I know. I'm sorry. Come for dinner tonight instead?"

"Tonight?"

"Jah."

He smiled broadly. "I'll be there." Slowly he placed her hand back down by her side, released it, and then turned and walked away. She stood and watched him leave. A few steps later, he turned around and gave her a wave. She waved in reply, and then hurried back to the stall.

"You're in love," Honor said when Joy got back.

"I think I am. I can't imagine feeling more for anyone than I do for him. I feel so good when he's around. I feel as though I come alive, and when he's gone I feel as though I'm not really living. Is that crazy?"

"*Jah.* It is. Now you know how I feel about Jonathon."

"*Nee,* it's nothing like it. The difference between you and me is that I wouldn't run away."

"I know that—because you're perfect." Honor rolled her eyes.

Joy didn't want to start an argument and she already regretted what she'd said. "I didn't say I was perfect, but I do try to do the right thing as much as possible." Joy flipped her *kapp* strings over her shoulders as though she was shrugging off her earlier words.

"What if running away was your only option to stop you from losing Isaac forever? What would you do? Choose your family or Isaac?"

Joy scoffed. "It was more like, choose the community or go with your boyfriend. No, wait a minute. You *did* leave the community to go with your boyfriend."

"Stop it." Honor glared at her and then her fingertips quickly covered a yawn.

"Ha! You're tired because you spent most of the night speaking with Jonathon. I heard you. It was like one o'clock in the morning when he left."

"*Nee.* Was it that late?"

"It was. I know it because I couldn't sleep with the two of

you talking. You should've told him to go because of us both having to wake up at four to get here in time."

"I couldn't do that. I'd miss sleep anytime to be with him for another moment."

Joy shook her head. "Just think of others, though."

"I can't help it if you're a light sleeper."

"You're lovesick," Joy said.

"So are you."

Joy rolled her eyes and just then some customers walked over to the stall and they had to end their conversation.

FLORENCE RARELY FOUND THE TIME TO WANDER THROUGH stores looking at what was for sale. There were always more important things to attend to. Now she and Ezekiel were at the crafts markets, and they were stopping to look at so many different things—jewelry, leather handbags and shoes, and all manner of handcrafted toys, and clothing, and candles ... the variety seemed endless.

Ezekiel couldn't make up his mind and after half an hour, Florence was tiring. "Do you have any idea at all what you're after?"

"Not really, I was kind of hoping you would know."

"I don't know what your mother would like, but I think

Ada would like something practical. Something she could use rather than something pretty to look at."

"Okay, well, that's a good start." They came across boot-cleaning kits in wooden boxes. "What about this?"

She took a step closer. "You've got brown polish there, and black polish, leather cream, brushes—everything you need. Who are you thinking of for that?"

"I don't know."

"It is practical."

"That's what I was thinking," Ezekiel said.

"I'm not sure who does the boot cleaning, though. It might be Samuel rather than Ada."

He put the kit back on the shelf with the others and looked at her. "Who does it in your family?"

"Mostly, we do our own."

He picked it back up. "I like it and if she likes practical things, she'll like this."

"Okay. That's one gift down."

He paid for it and it was handed to him in a large paper bag with string handles. "Where to now?"

"We'll keep going up and down the aisles until something jumps out at you for your *mudder*."

"Or something jumps out at you, since you're helping me."

"You were the one who spotted that present for Ada."

He chuckled. "I know, I quite surprised myself. What about this?" He reached out and took hold of a needlework cushion kit. "I like this." He held it up. It had the design already marked on the fabric and had needles and threads to go with it. "What do you think?"

"I like it too. The red and the green in the flowers will be quite striking. Do you think it'll be too bright for your *mudder?*"

"Nee. Everything else in the house is gray. This will brighten the place up and she loves this kind of thing."

She took a closer look and saw it was cross-stitch. "Are you positive?"

"Yes."

She laughed at the concentration on his face. "Get it, then."

"Okay, I will."

He paid for it and soon after that he got presents for his two brothers and a bunch of flowers for Wilma.

"How come Wilma got flowers?"

"Because she's a lovely lady and I'm thanking her for dinner last night."

"You don't have to do that."

"I like buying things for people. What about you?

Anything look good to you? I'll get you whatever you want."

"I don't need anything. In fact, I'll be quite upset if you get me anything. You bought me lunch, so there you go."

"Okay. I don't want you to get upset with me or you mightn't go out with me again."

She giggled at his comment. It made her feel good.

On the way out of the markets, he said, "Would you like to?"

Florence looked up at him. "Would I like to what?"

"Go out with me again?"

"Oh. *Jah,* I would. I'd like that." She surprised herself that she genuinely meant it. She wanted to see him again.

CHAPTER 7

*W*hen they got to Florence's house, he pulled up the buggy and looked over at her.

"Thank you for coming out with me today, Florence. Would you be free to do something with me tomorrow?"

"Sure."

He rubbed his chin. "I gave my word I'd help Samuel with rebuilding a chimney at Simon Miller house, but that might not take long."

"Simon? His *fraa*, Liza's my best friend. I'd love to come along. I didn't know there was anything wrong with their chimney."

"It's stone and it's crumbling away in pieces. How about I collect you around nine and we can go together?"

"Nine in the morning sounds perfect. I'll call Liza from

the phone in the barn and make sure she's going to be home."

"Samuel said she'd be supplying us with refreshments."

"Wunderbaar. I don't even need to call."

He smiled at her. "I better get Wilma's flowers out and give them to her."

"She'll be delighted. She loves flowers in the house when our garden is in bloom."

Florence climbed out of the buggy and together they walked up to the house. She pushed open the front door and then looked around for her stepmother. "I'll have to look in the kitchen."

Right then, Wilma came out of the kitchen wiping her hands on a towel. "Oh! I wasn't expecting you home quite so early."

"Is it early? It feels like we've had a long day." She quickly added, "I mean, because we fitted so much in," not wanting him to think she'd been bored.

"It's only four o'clock," Wilma said.

He held the flowers out to her. "These are for you, Wilma.
"

"For me?"

"Yes."

"Oh, that's very kind." She took the bunch from him, and

stared at the daisies mixed with pink and burgundy lilies, and a scattering of deeper pink roses. "I can't remember the last time anyone brought me flowers." She took them from him. *"Denke.* I'll just put these in some water. Come into the kitchen and I'll make you both *kaffe."* They followed her in and sat down and then she turned to face them with the teakettle in her hands. "You will be staying for dinner, won't you, Ezekiel?"

"I can't tonight, I'm sorry. Ada has the bishop and his *fraa* coming for the evening meal. It's a good chance for me to meet him before the meeting on Sunday."

"Jah, quite right." Wilma turned back and put the kettle on the stove.

Then she sat down with them. "Tell me, what have you been doing today?"

"I wanted to get a few things. Florence has been so kind as to show me around the markets."

"Oh, that's good. Is that all you did?"

Florence could tell Wilma liked Ezekiel by the way she was talking. "We also had lunch at one of the cafes and I think that's all." Wilma's obvious approval made Florence more comfortable with him. Now she felt like she was one half of a couple. It was a nice feeling to have. "Where is everyone?" Florence noticed the absence of Favor and Hope.

"I've got them working upstairs cleaning the windows."

"That's good. Does that mean everything on the list is finished?"

"All the cooking that needed to be done has been done. And we can always do more after dinner if the girls come home and tell us they're short of something."

"Of course."

"Sounds like you've got a highly organized team here, Wilma."

"We have to be highly organized. Otherwise nothing would get done," Wilma said.

"That's right." Florence agreed. "The girls would just stand around talking to each other and laughing all the daylong if we didn't have a plan and a routine to follow."

"It's good that they all get along so well."

Florence and *Mamm* exchanged smiles. "Most of the time they do," Florence said.

Once he had finished his coffee, Ezekiel was ready to leave. Florence walked him out to his buggy. As she stood watching him drive away, she realized if she'd written down a list of the qualities she needed in a man, he would've fulfilled every one of them.

CHAPTER 8

*N*ow that her big day with Ezekiel was over, Florence figured she had about twenty minutes of daylight left. She walked back into the house, took hold of her warm hand-knitted shawl, threw it around her shoulders, and then skipped down the porch steps. It had been a big day with Ezekiel and she'd enjoyed it, but at the same time being with one person all day had been a little overwhelming.

When she reached the first row of trees, the soft outline of the moon had already appeared in the pale gray sky. As she walked between the rows of apple trees, many scenarios about her potential future with Ezekiel played out in her mind. Then her thoughts turned to her parents. What guidance would they have given if they'd been alive?

"Florence."

Florence was jolted from her daydreams. It was Carter's

voice. She was nearly at the border of her property and his.

"Hello," she called out to him as he leaned on the wooden fence post that held five strands of wire to keep his cattle on his side of the property line.

"How are you?"

"Fine." She walked closer, knowing he wanted to talk.

When she was a few feet away, he began, "I was sitting in my kitchen—my *new* kitchen—and when I looked out the window I saw you."

She frowned when he stopped at that. "You saw me where?"

"In a buggy. But, it wasn't your buggy. I know the two horses you use and it wasn't either of those. A man was driving it, which also led me to the conclusion it wasn't your buggy."

"Ah, that would've been Ezekiel."

He stood up straight, and now one hand rested lightly atop the post.

She wished he wasn't so handsome. Even in old jeans and a pullover he looked good. His hair had been cut short—which, she noted in her musings, particularly suited him.

"A friend of yours?"

"Yes. A new friend. He's a farmer."

"What kind of a farm does he have?"

She had been so hoping he wouldn't ask that question. "A pig farm."

"He's hardly suited to be your friend since you don't have any pigs. Does he have anything to do with apples?"

"I don't think so, apart from liking to eat them. I met him recently."

"Yes, you said that already."

"He's from another community. It's not too far away."

He slowly nodded while not taking his eyes from hers. "Are you going to marry this man who spends his day with pigs?"

She tried not to laugh at the expression on his face. It was half disgust and half shock. "It's a bit soon to think about things like that."

His eyebrows rose. "Is it? One of your sisters married someone not too long ago and then there's Honor, the escapee. We both know she fled the scene when she wasn't allowed to marry the man she loves. Even though he was a jerk, I'm sure her feelings were real."

Secretly she was pleased he held the same opinion of Jonathon as her own. "It wasn't that she 'wasn't allowed.' She will be allowed when she's older."

"I'm not talking about them, I'm talking about you." He shook his head. "Tell me you're not in love with a pig farmer." His lips were open just slightly as though he was about to say something else.

Was he jealous? It didn't matter. It couldn't matter. There was no point stringing him along. She could never be with a man like him, so whatever was between them had to stop. This seemed like a *Gott*-given opportunity to end their friendship in case it developed into more. "Who knows? I might end up marrying him. We're very similar in many ways."

He tilted his head to one side. "How so?"

"He works with his family on his farm just as I work with my family on the orchard. His farm is as important to him as my orchard is to me."

"And that's a basis for marriage? If that were the case you'd be suited to every unmarried farmer in the whole countryside and beyond."

"Well … he's Amish, too."

He ignored that comment, which was—in all honesty— her main point, and looked over at his cows placidly eating their hay. "How can someone be around animals and then slaughter them for food?" He shook his head and looked down.

"He treats his pigs humanely. They wander the fields and …"

He raised his hand to stop her there. "I'd rather not think about it."

"It's because you're from the city. If you'd been raised in the country, you wouldn't think twice about it. It seems you city-folk don't even know where your food comes from. You wouldn't survive a day if you were suddenly thrust into the wilds of a forest."

He pressed his lips together hard. "How would it work if you married him? Would you have to be subservient and leave your apple trees?"

That was a concern. It would've been much easier to find a man in her area, so if she couldn't live on the land of the orchard, she'd maybe still have the chance to be there every day. "If it's God's will, He'll work things out."

"You're leaving your future to *chance?*"

From his comment, and from his aghast expression, she knew he had no belief whatsoever in God. Her mouth opened, and then she closed it. She had words, but they were many and all jumbled up, and there was no point getting into a discussion with him. He was too opinionated and, she guessed, narrow-minded.

Then he waved a hand in the air dismissing their previous conversation. "All that aside, why have you been avoiding me?"

CHAPTER 9

"*I* haven't been avoiding you." Her tongue made the denial before she had a chance to realize she wasn't being honest.

"I never see you anymore."

Feeling she was choking, she loosened her prayer *kapp* strings underneath her chin. "I've been busy."

"With what?" he shot back.

"Oh, just the usual things that need to be done around the place." He often talked about them having no man there, so she used that. "As you know there's no man around the house, so I'm the one who has to do all the odd jobs and there are a lot of those."

He grinned, softening his face and, she hoped, his mood too. "Is there anything you can't do?"

She relaxed a little. "There are many things I can't do."

"But I'd reckon you'd learn pretty quickly if the need arose. I can see a lot of determination in the startling depths of those blue eyes."

Another compliment. It pleased her, but she wasn't going to allow him to see it. "What have *you* been doing lately?" She hoped she'd find out about that woman she'd seen there the other day. Nodding toward his house, she added, "Have you done any more renovations?"

"After talking to you about that, I decided to put things on hold. I agree with you about keeping the old character of the place. They say every house has a soul and each person who lives in it contributes a little piece of themselves."

Slowly, she nodded at his ramblings. That ruled out the woman being any kind of consultant for the renovations, or an interior designer. "What part of yourself have you contributed?"

He chuckled. "I've added some soul of the city. Physically, a little bit of modernization, and in turn it's breathed new life into it so it can keep breathing new life."

She frowned wondering if that made sense. *He's adding physical things and calls that a soul?*

"How's your wayward sister?" he asked, before she could respond about his house.

Florence giggled. "Which one?"

"The one that was sent away in disgrace. Not the runaway."

"Oh, Cherish—she's fine, I think. She writes to Mom every other day, pleading to come home."

The smile left his face. "That's heart-breaking."

"No, it's not!" She shook her head. "If you knew her you wouldn't think so."

"It seems harsh. Why can't the girl come home if she's having such a miserable time?"

"She did some things she shouldn't have done and would've gotten herself into big trouble if we didn't do something drastic. She tried to run away. It seems she had a crush on the same man as Honor and she was on her way to find him."

He threw his head back and laughed. "You've had two runaways?"

"We have."

"It must've been a hard decision—which one to send away. The thing you must be concerned about, though, is why they don't want to stay."

Her fingertips flew to her mouth. She'd never considered that. Was home-life so dreadful for her sisters they saw marriage as their only escape? "There's a simple answer.

They want to grow up too fast. Oh, and something else you don't know. Jonathon is back and he's apologized."

"That's the one I met when I drove you to get Honor?"

Florence nodded.

"Just like that, everything's okay? He's been forgiven, just like that?"

When Florence nodded, confusion covered his face and she was pleased that he felt the same as she. "Well, my mother has now said they can marry when she turns eighteen. They have to wait nearly a year."

He shook his head. "Is that your stepmother?"

She nodded. "Yes, that's right."

"Hmmm. Seems odd that she'd reward them for what they did."

"It's not like that. She figures when Honor's eighteen, she won't be able to stand in their way so it's better to give her blessing, with that limitation. By telling them they're approved of, they won't feel the need to run away again. At least, I'm sure that's what she's thinking."

"How old were you when your mother died? If you don't mind me asking."

"I was only two, and she died from heart inflammation caused by some kind of virus. My father was left with me and my two older brothers."

"I'm sorry. That's terribly sad."

"I don't remember much about her, which is also sad. Two years later, my father married Wilma."

"And they went on to have six girls together," he said.

"That's right. I remember I was pleased to have a mother because I wanted to be carried all the time." She smiled at the hazy memory. "Wilma carried me around on her hip and that kept me happy."

He smiled as he once again leaned on the wooden fencepost. "She wouldn't have been able to carry you for long though, because those bonnet sisters would've been arriving thick and fast if there are six of them."

"Don't call us that."

"I was calling them that, not you."

She sighed.

"Okay. I'm sorry."

She realized it was happening again. He was making her talk about herself and she still didn't know anything about him. "You haven't told me anything about your family."

The smile left his face and he took his arm off the fence. "There's nothing to tell."

"Oh really? So, you just appeared in the vegetable patch one dark and stormy night? Maybe a beanstalk dropped you?"

"That's right. Dropped me from a great height and I

landed on my head." He tapped his head with his knuckles.

She giggled, and then said, "Seriously, Carter, tell me about your family. I've told you lots about mine."

He shrugged his shoulders and then his lips slightly curved upward. "Okay, I've got nothing to hide. I was an only child and never saw much of my parents. I told you that before."

"I don't think so. You only said you were by yourself and that could mean many things. Anyway, why didn't you see much of your parents?"

"It's a long story." He grinned. "I might even tell you about it one day."

"There's a saying that I like. Never put off till tomorrow what you can do today."

He ran a hand over his cropped dark hair. "I don't want to bore you."

"Unfair. You know everything about me and I know very little about you."

His eyebrows raised. "You'd like to know more about me?"

"Well, you live next door and we're neighbors, so yes. I'd like to know who's living in the house my father once owned."

"What do you want to know?"

"Do you have a job?"

"Not a job as such. It's difficult to explain."

"I'm sure I'll understand. I do read the newspapers sometimes. I'm not totally cut-off from what's happening in the world. I know there are jobs people do off-site without turning up to an office every day." She took a stab in the dark. "Do you do something from home on your computer?" Out of the corner of her eye, she saw movement. A car was coming up his driveway. He looked around and saw it too.

"I have a visitor, it seems," he mumbled, looking none too happy to see the car.

Florence stared at the car's occupant. She was certain it was the same woman from the other day. "A member of your family?"

"No. Excuse me, Florence, I'll have to speak with her."

"Sure. That's fine."

He took two steps away and then swung around. "Will you come back tomorrow?"

She shrugged her shoulders. "I walk most days. It just depends which way I go." He kept glancing over his shoulder, preoccupied rather than listening to her. "Bye, Carter."

He faced her and gave her a quick smile. "Bye, Florence."

She walked back to the safety of her apple trees

grumbling about the bad timing of that woman. He'd been just about to tell her what he did for a living. When she reached the first tree, she looked back. The woman was out of the car and they were talking. He said something to her and then they walked into the house. If she wasn't someone to do with his renovations, and she wasn't a relative ... *hmmm ...someone from his work, perhaps?*

CHAPTER 10

*M*eanwhile, Joy and Honor were driving home from the markets in the buggy.

"I think I forgot to ask Florence if Isaac can come to dinner tonight."

"It'll be fine. I can't see why it wouldn't be. I won't be there, so there'll be one less place at the table." She giggled. "One less mouth to feed."

"Where are you going?"

"Out with Jonathon. Where else would I go?"

"Do Florence or *Mamm* know that?"

"I'm not sure. I told *Mamm*, but I never know if she's paying attention. Why? Do you think Florence will mind?"

"It's hard to say. I don't know what she'll be mad at any

more. I don't think she's ever been mad at me." Joy giggled.

"That's because you always do what they want you to do."

"No, I do what I want to do and it just so happens to be that they don't mind me doing that."

"You wouldn't do anything wrong anyway. So no one will ever be upset with you."

"Good. Because that's the way I like it. Why would I want to upset anyone?"

Honor shook her head. "Don't worry. There are some things that you just don't understand."

"What kind of things?"

"The kind of things like, how it feels to be in love."

"I like Isaac a lot."

"Jah, but are you in love with him?"

"You were the one who said I was earlier today. How would I know the difference?"

"If you have to ask that you're not in love with him."

"How can you say that? You don't know what's in my heart."

"Sounds like you could live without him. That means it's not the same love that Jonathon and I have. Ours is so strong."

Joy didn't want to get into an argument over whose relationship was better, so she changed the subject. "What do you think about Ezekiel?"

"I think he's lovely. He'll suit Florence fine."

"But what'll happen if Florence leaves? We need her around. *Mamm* needs her, everyone needs her. She runs the place."

"She won't leave, silly. There's no way she would."

When they got to the bottom of the driveway, they saw Jonathon standing beside his buggy next to their barn.

"What's he doing?" Joy stared at Honor.

"We're going somewhere."

"Oh, right now? Why didn't you tell me that? I thought you meant later on."

"Sorry. *Mamm* said it was okay, if that's your next question, so I hope she remembers it. Can you do me a favor and unhitch the buggy so I can leave sooner?"

"Sure."

"*Denke.*"

Florence came home from her walk just in time to see Honor riding off with Jonathon. She walked over to Joy, who was rubbing down the horse.

"Where are they going?"

Joy looked up and then glanced over her shoulder at the fast-disappearing buggy. "I don't know where they're heading, but I do know *Mamm* said it was okay."

"And Honor's left you to unhitch the buggy?"

"I don't mind. Truly I don't."

"I'll help you." As Florence moved closer, she asked, "You're not planning to run away too, are you?"

"Of course not. Can Isaac come for dinner tonight?"

"Of course."

"Good. I invited him already."

Florence giggled. They often had people stopping by for dinner, so one extra wasn't ever an issue. They always cooked plenty.

When they had put the buggy undercover and finished caring for the horse, they walked into the mudroom together. They changed their shoes and washed up, and headed through to the kitchen. "

Florence thought it best to check Joy's story with *Mamm.* "*Mamm,* did you say it was okay for Honor to go somewhere with Jonathon?"

"I did. Why, is there something wrong?"

"I suppose not. If you said it was all right."

Mamm softly laid a hand on Florence's shoulder. "We have to trust them."

"Do we?"

Joy knew she wasn't part of the conversation, but still she couldn't help butting in. "If you allow them freedom they won't feel they have to run away."

Florence shot her a look that told her to be quiet. "Do you want help with dinner, *Mamm?*"

"Favor and Hope have already done that."

"Great, what is it? I'm starving."

"Joy, you completely butted in and I wasn't finished with what I was saying."

Joy huffed. "I'm sorry."

"Mamm, don't you think there should be some restrictions placed upon them?"

Mamm stared at her without blinking. "Do you think so?"

"I do."

"Okay, we'll talk about it after dinner."

"We can't because Isaac will be here," Joy said.

Mamm looked up in shock. "I thought it was just us tonight! He's coming again?"

"Jah," Florence and Joy chorused.

"When will Honor be home?" Florence asked *Mamm.*

"They're going to have dinner at Christina and Mark's house."

That made Florence feel a little better.

"I don't know why they invite her over all the time. What about us?" Joy asked.

Mamm nodded. "I know. Christina has always gotten along well with Honor."

Joy tilted her head upward. "I don't know why she can't get along with all of us and treat all of us the same."

Florence yawned. "I might have a little lie down before dinner. Is that okay with everyone?"

Mamm's eyes opened wide as she looked at Florence. "You're not getting sick, are you?"

"Nee. I'm not used to all the shopping I've done today. I'm exhausted."

Joy giggled. "You can work from sunup to sundown at harvest time and you're exhausted over a little shopping?"

Florence shrugged her shoulders. "I guess it does sound funny."

"I'll fetch you when dinner's on the table," *Mamm* said.

"Denke."

Florence climbed the stairs feeling pretty awful. The trouble was, she liked everything in her life to be organized and that meant having a fair idea about her future so she could plan. Now, her future was uncertain.

Carter was right, how could she have a future with

Ezekiel when they lived so far apart? And even if there wasn't that problem, she wasn't in love with Ezekiel.

She pushed open her bedroom door with the edge of her boot. Was she only attracted to Carter because he brought some excitement into her life, along with a hint of the unknown? Maybe she liked the danger that being fond of an *Englischer* brought.

CHAPTER 11

After they'd had dinner and Isaac had gone home, Joy made use of the time before bed to make taffy apples for the next day. They were completely sold out of them at the markets.

Joy was in the midst of warming the toffee when Jonathon brought Honor home. Jonathon came inside with her, and then Joy heard him ask to speak with *Mamm* and Florence. Hope and Favor were upstairs and with the quiet surrounding her, she was able to hear every word of the conversation that was happening in the living room.

"The problem is, he hasn't been able to find work around here," said Honor.

Joy frowned at his excuse. He hadn't been looking for long.

"I wouldn't worry. Something will happen soon," *Mamm* said.

Florence wasn't so placid. "How long's it been? Only two weeks? Surely there's something out there you could do. It doesn't have to be your ideal job."

Joy covered her mouth to stifle a giggle; Florence had said exactly what she'd thought.

"Believe me, Florence, I don't like having time on my hands. I've done everything I can and left my name at so many places. Samuel and Mark have been asking around for me too."

"Tell them what we talked about, Jonathon," Honor urged.

There was a moment of silence. Joy stopped skewering the apples so she would be able to hear Jonathon better.

"I've been offered a job near my folks' place. This job is secure—it's with one of my uncles. I've talked with my parents and they said they'd love to have Honor stay there. Even though Mercy and Stephen are there. There's still plenty of room."

"Wait! Wait a minute. What are you suggesting?" Florence asked.

Joy put down the apple that was in her hand. She never imagined he'd ask such a thing. Before he could answer Florence, *Mamm* spoke.

"And where will *you* stay if we allow Honor to board with your parents?"

Joy couldn't resist it. She tiptoed over to the doorway of the kitchen and peeped around the corner.

Florence stared at *Mamm* in disbelief. Was *Mamm* going to allow them both to leave just like that? After everything that had just happened?

Joy shook her head, sympathizing with Florence. She had no real say when Mamm overrode any of her decisions.

"I was thinking that I'll stay with friends. There are plenty of people I can stay with."

Joy knew exactly what Florence was thinking. As she sat in stunned silence, Florence was hoping *Mamm* wasn't seriously considering the option of Honor leaving to be close to Jonathon with only his parents to supervise.

Mamm then stared at Florence. "What do you think?"

When all eyes were on her, Florence had to say what she thought. *"Nee!* I don't think it's a good idea." She looked directly at Jonathon. "I'm a little shocked you've asked us something like this, Jonathon, after everything you've put us through already."

"Why, Florence?" Honor asked.

"It's simply out of the question. Both of you ran away and I don't trust either of you now."

Joy knew they'd be short another pair of hands if Honor left. It was more difficult with two of her sisters gone, and it would be harder still if they were down a third.

"Mamm?" Honor asked through tear-filled eyes.

"We'll have to think about it."

"There's no time to think."

"It's okay, don't get upset." Jonathon patted Honor's shoulder. Tears flowed down Honor's face and she bounded to her feet and left the room. Jonathon stood up and stared after her as she ran up the stairs. Then, he slowly sat down. "Florence, I have a job there and she'll be perfectly safe with my folks. They're even stricter than you."

"All the same, I've given my answer."

He looked at *Mamm.* "Mrs. Baker? You said you'd think about it."

Joy hoped her mother would back Florence up.

Mamm stood up. "Just one moment. I'll talk to Honor and see how she's feeling."

Mamm was going to be talked into allowing it. Joy just knew it. She always caved under pressure.

"I'm not the way you think I am," Jonathon told Florence now that they were left alone.

"Would you like a cup of hot tea?"

Joy frowned at Florence's strange response. What did tea have to do with anything?

"I wouldn't mind a *kaffe,*" he answered.

"Sure." She stood and then he got up to follow her into the kitchen. *"Nee.* You sit down."

"I thought we could talk."

"Nee. I've said all I have to say about the matter."

"We could talk about something else then."

She stared at him and shook her head, and then he slowly sat back down.

Joy ducked away, turned down the stove, and then sat down and pretended to continue skewering the apples even though she'd finished.

Florence saw her and stopped, then walked to the teakettle and filled it with water.

"I'm making taffy apples."

"So I see." Florence then lit another burner on the stove and placed the teakettle on it, next to the pot of toffee.

Joy rushed over to her and whispered, "I heard everything. I wasn't deliberately listening—I was kind of stuck in here. What's your main objection to what they asked?"

Florence sighed. "She was told that she couldn't marry him until she was eighteen. It only feels like they've been back days from running away. We might never have seen them again, and now they want us to forget everything and trust them. *Nee,* trust must be earned. Especially with having done what they did."

Joy placed her hands down by her sides as she wandered back to the kitchen table and played with her apples. "Part of me agrees, but the other part doesn't. What about forgiveness?" She looked back at Florence.

"Let's get these apples dipped while we're waiting for the kettle to boil."

"Okay, *denke.* But I'm serious. What about forgiveness— shouldn't that mean we let go of it?"

"There is forgiveness, and there's bringing up a child correctly. You can forgive, but you still have to give guidance. Do you see what I mean?"

"Sort of, but Honor isn't ten-years-old. She's an adult and she told me she's old enough to get married if she has a parent's permission, so why not let *Mamm* give it if they love each other? Their love must've been strong to feel the need to turn their backs on both of their families just so they could be together." Joy could see both sides of the issue.

Florence shook her head. "I'm not about to forget what they did. She can't just say she's sorry and then all is forgiven and forgotten, and the same with him. You'll know what it's like when you have your own *kinner* to raise."

"So might you. None of us is your *kinner,* Florence. You're our *schweschder.*"

"Half-*schweschder,* as I'm so often reminded."

"And I know you do pretty much everything around here, but the end decision lies with *Mamm.*"

Joy saw Florence's face change, and she regretted her words. "I'm sorry. I didn't mean that like it came out."

"That's okay. You're right—I'm just frustrated. *Mamm* could very easily give in and allow Honor to do whatever she wants. We'll just have to wait and see what *Mamm* says."

Joy quickly turned away. It couldn't have been easy for Florence, trying to get all the girls in the family to behave well. "How are things between you and Ezekiel?"

"We're doing okay. Getting to know one another. I can see the two of us will be good friends."

"And that's good, isn't it? Don't friends make the best husbands?"

"Well, that's something I can't really say because I have had no experience with that."

"I can see the two of you together having lots of *bopplis.*"

Florence smiled. "Well, that's fine. As for you, don't think you have to rush in just because Mercy and Honor have made their choices early in life."

"Why? Don't you like Isaac?"

"I do. Very much. I think very highly of him, but at your age, you have all the time in the world. Use it wisely."

. . .

BY THE TIME *MAMM* CAME BACK DOWNSTAIRS, THE APPLES had been finished and Florence had just served Jonathon his cup of coffee.

"Here's a hot tea for you, *Mamm,*" Joy said.

"*Denke*, Joy. Um ... Joy, do you mind if Florence and I have a talk alone with Jonathon?"

"Sure. I mean, no, I don't mind. I was just going to bed anyway." Joy took her own cup of hot tea upstairs while Florence sat down on the couch next to Jonathon and opposite *Mamm.*

"Have you made a decision yet?" Jonathon asked.

"*Jah.* I've decided she can go with you, but I'll have to speak to your parents first to make sure it's all going to be okay."

Florence stared at Jonathon in shock. He'd gotten just what he wanted and he smirked as though he was pleased with himself.

"*Denke*, Mrs. Baker."

Florence stood.

"Where are you going?" *Mamm* said.

"I'm following Joy. I'm going up to bed. Good night, all."

"But aren't you going to stay and talk about this?" *Mamm* asked, staring up at her.

Florence sighed. "There's nothing more to say."

Florence leaned forward and picked up her cup and saucer and then balanced them carefully while walking up the stairs to her bedroom.

As she sat on her bed sipping her tea, she decided she should worry less about the girls and start thinking more about herself. Tomorrow, she was going to seriously consider Ezekiel Troyer as a potential husband, even more so than she had thus far.

CHAPTER 12

The next morning, Florence rubbed her eyes trying her best to forget a lost night's sleep due to worry over what might become of Honor. She'd done pretty poorly at sticking to her resolve to worry less about her half-sisters.

Florence had to wait until after breakfast to be alone with *Mamm* so she could tell her what she thought. No one had mentioned anything about Honor and Jonathon the entire morning. Both Honor and *Mamm* had avoided eye-contact with her.

"I honestly can't believe you, *Mamm.* You're rewarding them for running away."

Mamm nodded. "I know you're upset."

"I am, and it all started when Honor ran away. You left with Cherish without even bothering to punish Honor properly. It was left up to me to give her extra chores. If

Honor had been given a harsher punishment, she might've seen things clearly. Now Jonathon's weaseled his way around the situation and gotten his way."

"What you don't know is that something else might've happened. That's why I didn't punish her for returning. If she's punished for coming home, she might not come home the next time."

Florence frowned wondering which way was right.

"We've had a win. She's stayed here and they've asked permission rather than doing things their own way like last time. Now, don't get upset, but there's something else I haven't told you. I told all the girls this morning but I told them that I wanted to tell you myself."

Florence stared at her stepmother. Had someone died? "What is it?"

"After you went to bed last night, I had a more serious talk with Jonathon and I gave them permission to marry. So, they'll marry before he leaves to take that job."

At first, Florence thought she hadn't heard correctly. "What?" She put her hand over her heart to calm herself as she wrapped her mind around the shocking news. While her stepmother repeated it, Florence pulled out a chair and sat down. "I can't believe what I'm hearing. This was everything I was trying to avoid." She shook her head. "Now I feel I wasted my time bringing her back. I should've just let them run away."

"*Nee,* you did the right thing. Now they're staying in the community and they would've left if you'd hadn't brought her back here."

Florence rounded her shoulders in defeat. "I'm shocked, but still, I know it's not my decision to make." It was deeply upsetting that her opinions were so disregarded by *Mamm.* She felt like she truly *was* wasting her time. All she wanted to do now was get far away from the house so the news could sink in. "So, you're serious about this? They're actually getting married?"

"*Jah.* They're visiting the bishop today to arrange a date for their baptisms and for their wedding, as soon as he'll permit."

With a hand over her stomach, mentally fighting the nausea, she looked at the half-made apple pies. "Once these pies are in the oven, I'll visit Liza."

"I can do the rest if you want to go now."

"*Denke,* but Ezekiel is collecting me at nine to take me there. He's volunteered with some other men to fix Samuel and Liza's chimney."

Mamm nodded. "You look over-worked. You probably need some time with your friend."

"*Denke, Mamm.*"

Florence couldn't wait to leave all her problems behind her. Liza was a good listener and she always agreed with Florence's way of thinking. Complaining to her best friend was all that she'd need to make her feel better.

When she saw Ezekiel's borrowed buggy coming toward the house, she hurried out to meet him. The first thing she noticed was his big smile.

"Wie gehts?" he asked.

"I'm good, and you?"

"Fine, on such a beautiful morning."

The sky was gray and a chilling wind swept through the orchard. It was anything but beautiful. She climbed into the buggy next to him. "Are you looking forward to the day ahead?"

"I am. I helped work on a chimney not long ago, so I do have some experience."

As the horse clip-clopped along the road, their relaxed conversation continued, allowing Florence to release some of the tension her home-life so often brought.

When they pulled up at Liza and Simon's house, Liza was waiting at the door. Florence stepped down and walked to meet her while Ezekiel secured the horse.

"I'm so pleased you're here because I've been wanting to tell you this for days." Liza then glanced across at Ezekiel. "Oh! Hello. I didn't see you there."

Florence noticed Liza was unusually flustered.

"I'm here to help with the chimney," Ezekiel told her.

"Liza, this is Ezekiel Troyer."

"Pleased to meet you. *Denke* for coming to help. That's *wunderbaar.* The men are around the back."

"I hope I'm not late."

"Nee. They've only been here five minutes. I'll take you to them."

After they accompanied Ezekiel to where the men were just getting started, Liza looped her arm through Florence's and pulled her into the house through the back door.

"Now, what's this news?" Florence stared into her friend's face as they stood facing each other in the center of the kitchen. The glowing skin, her big smile and those sparkling eyes could only mean one thing. "You're having another *boppli?"*

She giggled. "I am"

The two women hugged. Florence was so overjoyed for her friend that it felt like something good had happened for her. This wasn't the right time to unburden all her worries. She'd hold them in for now. "That's so soon."

"I know. The two will be close together and we're hoping for another boy to be close in age with Malachi. Simon had Michael, and they were only a year apart."

Florence nodded as an image of Michael came into her mind, reminding her of his rejection of her.

"I'm sorry, I shouldn't have mentioned Michael."

"Nee, that's okay. I'm over that now. I was over that a long time ago, believe me."

"I'm sure he didn't know you liked him. You should've let him know."

Florence shook her head. "That would've only made the inevitable rejection harder to bear."

"Oh, Florence, you shouldn't say that."

"That's all in the past. I'm so pleased for you. Your life's turning out just perfectly."

"I know, it is. Can I fix you some *kaffe?"*

"Please. I'd love a cup."

THE NOISE FROM THE BANGING AND HAMMERING IN THE living room was too loud, so Liza closed the door of the kitchen and they sat down with their coffee mugs at the kitchen table.

"Now, tell me about Ezekiel?"

"I spent the whole day with him yesterday."

"And, what do you think of him?"

"He's nice."

"Oh." Liza's shoulders dropped.

Florence laughed. "Nice, in a good way."

"Are you interested in him?"

Liza knew her better than anyone. "I haven't really gotten to know him yet. That's what I'm doing in the week that he's here." She sipped her hot coffee.

"That's good."

Florence placed her mug carefully down on the table. "He's very easy to be around."

"That's what you need. You need to marry someone who's also a friend."

"I guess so."

"I mean, most people go through rough patches in their marriage. It's mostly at the beginning when you're adjusting to one another."

Florence screwed up her nose. That part didn't sound like much fun.

"But, it's so worth it when you get through that bit," Liza added.

"Is that the same for everyone?"

"Most people. It's not easy sometimes."

"It should be easy. I want a love that's no effort whatsoever. A love where I don't have to work at it."

Liza laughed. "I hope you find it. You always complain about your sisters being unrealistic and now I know they get that from you."

Florence grimaced. *"Nee.* I'm a very practical person." She leaned forward and whispered, "I'm just hoping it works out with Ezekiel. It would be nice to have someone special in my life."

"And no one deserves it more than you. You're always doing everything for everyone else."

"When Earl and Mark moved away after *Dat* died, I had to assume the role as the oldest. Naturally, there's not much time to think about myself with running the orchard and everything."

"The orchard, the shop, the household and everything else. I hope they appreciate you."

Florence wasn't doing it for appreciation. She was doing it because that was what needed to be done.

"If Ezekiel's right for you, it'll happen." Liza took a mouthful of coffee.

"That's true. Oh, Liza, I'm so pleased for you. You waited long enough for your first *boppli* and now to have another one straight after, you must be thrilled."

"I am. It's *wunderbaar,* and Simon's ... well he just doesn't have words to express himself, but he cried when I told him."

Florence laughed. "I hope they were happy tears."

"Most definitely, tears of joy." The two of them shared a little chuckle. "I have something to ask you."

"What's that?"

"Will you be there at the birth, to help me?"

Florence was delighted she asked. "Really?"

"Jah, I'd love it if you would."

"I'd love to."

"Denke. I was going to ask you last time, but my *schweschder*-in-law pushed her way in and volunteered. I didn't want too many people there. This time, I'm getting in first with you, and I'll tell her no."

"I'd be truly honored to be there to share your special moment. I can't think of anything I'd like more. I'd love it." Liza felt closer to her than any of her own half-sisters did.

When Florence left Liza's, she rode homeward in the buggy beside Ezekiel, her mind full of mixed feelings. She'd gone there to unburden her woes. She wasn't expecting Liza's good news – news that brought home to her what her own life had become.

She glanced over at Ezekiel who seemed much quieter than usual. "Are you tired?"

"Very. It was hard work."

That was all he said. He seemed to be in a funny mood and Florence couldn't work out why. Perhaps he was just tired.

CHAPTER 13

*A*cross town, Joy and Hope were serving at their stall at the farmers market. Hope left to get a mid-afternoon take-out coffee, leaving her sister at the stall alone.

Joy was busy serving a customer. She took the money and then handed her customer a bag containing two jars of pickles and a jar of apple sauce. Once the customer left, she noticed her friend Bliss Bruner was standing close by. There was a quiet moment between customers, so she waved Bliss over.

Before even saying hello, Bliss said, "Did you realize my *vadder* likes your *mudder?*"

Joy'd had her suspicions about that ever since Levi Bruner had gifted their family Wilbur—a fine gelding. If her mother felt the same about him, Joy wasn't sure how she herself would feel about a stepfather. "Really? He likes her?"

"*Jah.* He didn't admit it, but he talks about her an awful lot and what a *wunderbaar* woman she is." Bliss laughed. "Do you think they'd make a good pair?"

"I don't know, I have to think about it a bit more."

"I've been thinking about it."

Joy laughed.

"What if we arrange something where they could spend some more time alone?"

Joy winced. She didn't want to interfere. Her mother had never shown any interest in men apart from *Dat.* Still, she didn't feel she could say no. Bliss seemed so excited. "What did you have in mind?"

"Maybe, a dinner. What if just your *mudder* comes to my place for dinner, and then I'll leave them alone?"

That sounded awful. "That would be a little obvious, don't you think?"

"*Nee.*"

"I don't think she'd like it. It'd make her feel awkward, and she might think your *vadder* arranged it."

"Does she even want to get married again?"

"I don't think so, Bliss." Joy shook her head. "She's never talked about it." Joy didn't know if she or any of her sisters was ready to have a stepfather. "I really don't think we should do anything. If it's meant to be, and if *Gott* wants it to happen, it will." She smiled at Bliss, hoping she'd see the sense in that.

Bliss giggled. "Yeah, but it won't matter if we help it along a bit, will it?"

"I'm not comfortable with that," Joy said.

"Why not? You were a moment ago."

"Now I've had time to think about it, though, and I'm not interested in interfering."

More customers approached the counter, and Bliss stepped back. Once the customers left, Bliss carried on talking. "It will affect their lives, Joy, but only for the better. Aw, come on. You used to be more fun than this."

"Fun? I am fun. But this doesn't sound like fun to me."

Bliss blew out a deep breath. "I should've asked one of your sisters."

"Maybe it was just as well you didn't. I can't believe you think I'm not fun. I'm just the same as I always was."

"Don't you think it would be good if my *vadder* and your *mudder* got married?"

"Sure, if that's what they want. It would be great, but she's never spoken about marrying again." And then she had to know about Bliss's father. "Has your *vadder* mentioned anything about a second marriage?"

"Not so much. I mean, he talks about your *mudder*, but he

doesn't talk about marrying her." Bliss leaned forward. "Does she talk about him?"

"Nee, not really. Not like that." She couldn't remember her mother ever talking about him at all.

"Ach." The smile left Bliss's face.

"That could be because we've had so much going on with Mercy getting married and then Cherish going away. Now there's the Honor and Jonathon saga. Every day there seems to be some drama or other playing out."

"At least it sounds interesting." Bliss sighed. "Nothing ever happens at my place. It's boring with just me and *Dat."*

"'Boring?' You mean peaceful. Give me boring any day."

Bliss laughed. "I suppose it's all in the way you view it."

Joy nodded. "Anyway, it's interesting to know your *Dat* is sweet on *Mamm."*

"Don't you tell anyone. He'll be so upset with me."

"I won't say anything to *Mamm,* but I might tell one of my sisters—if that's okay? It's hard to keep things from them. Keeping any kind of a secret is not easy in our house."

"Okay."

"Here comes Hope now. About time. I can't do all this by myself. We're going to have the after-work crowd soon."

"I'll go. Bye now." Bliss hurried away before Joy could even say goodbye.

"What did she want?" Isaac frowned looking at Bliss striding away.

Joy was startled. She hadn't seen Isaac approaching from the other direction. "She just had some silly things she wanted me to be a part of."

"Like what?" Hope took a careful sip of her take-out coffee as she joined them.

Joy was now focused on coffee. She had thought Hope might've bought her one too. "Where's mine?"

"I thought you'd like to stretch your legs and get your own."

Joy grumbled.

"Take a walk with Isaac, but don't be too long."

"Unlike you, I won't." Joy took hold of her purse from under the counter and then Isaac and she walked away from the stall.

"Was Bliss talking about me?" he asked.

His question took her by surprise. "What? *Nee*, of course not. It wasn't about you. What makes you think that?"

"She left when she saw me coming. She's your friend and she probably doesn't think I'm good enough for you." He glanced over his shoulder, and then looked back at Joy. "Did she say something like that to you?"

She stared at Isaac. She'd never seen this side of him. "Why are you saying these things?"

"Things have never come easy for me, Joy. My size has always been an issue." He looked down at himself.

"There's nothing wrong with your size." He was only a little larger than others, and Joy liked the way he looked.

He patted his stomach. "I'm overweight. And when people see that, they think I'm lazy and not a hard worker. I've always been this way."

"She was talking about her *vadder* and my *mudder,* if you must know. I didn't want to say it, but she had the idea she and I should push them together."

Slowly, he nodded while studying her face. "If that's true, it sounds like meddling to me."

"Meddling ... yes, that's a good word. Sounds like it to me too. Hey, what do you mean by 'if that's true?' Of course it is. Why would I say something untrue to you?"

"I'm sorry."

"It's okay. I guess you've heard the news about Honor and Jonathon? The shocking news, I should say."

"Jah, Jonathon mentioned they're getting married. I was there when he told Mark and Christina."

"I'm a little shocked, but anyway, that ruins your plan of moving out with him. They're moving away, too. Heading back to Wisconsin. I forget what the Amish community there is called."

"Jah. He told me all that—but I don't recall the name of

their community either." He rubbed his chin. "Do you want coffee?"

"Not now. Let's just walk around. Talking about Honor getting married has made me feel a little sick. I've gone from five sisters to two in just a couple of months. Not counting Florence, that is."

"Big changes for you."

She sighed. "It makes me feel uneasy somehow."

"In what way?"

"I just want things the way they were before Stephen appeared. He took Mercy away. It was only supposed to be for a year, but there's no sign of them returning."

Isaac nodded. "That's the thing about life, things never stay the same. Everything is always changing and there's nothing much we can do about it."

"I guess."

"Do they have a date for the wedding? Jonathon didn't say."

"I don't know, but I think it's going to be soon because Jonathon has to start work back home." She shook her head. "I can't believe *Mamm* allowed this."

"Aren't you happy for Honor?"

"Not really, if I'm honest."

He opened his mouth in shock. "Why not?"

"I think she should've waited to see if someone else came along that she'd like better."

He stared at her in disbelief and then looked down. When they had walked another couple of paces, he asked, "Is that what you're doing with me?"

"We'll just have to wait and see what happens."

"I need some kind of assurance of your feelings. Can't you give me that?"

Joy didn't like being put on the spot. Was he asking if she intended marrying him? That was something she'd think about in a few years, not now. "I'm way too young to get married now and I don't think I'll be ready to marry when I'm seventeen or even eighteen. I want to be fully grown up and ready to make a responsible decision." That's what Florence was always telling her and her sisters and she wanted to do the right thing. After all, among the Amish, marriage was for life.

He slowly nodded. "So where do things stand with us?"

"I like you, otherwise I wouldn't be spending so much time with you. I'm just being honest right now."

He shook his head. "I know what the problem is. And it's a problem I can't do anything about." He stopped still, and then left her there and walked away in the other direction.

"Wait!" She caught up with him and touched his arm and he stopped. "What's the matter?" When Isaac turned to face her, she saw how upset he was. "Why are you acting so strange today?"

He frowned and took a step away from her. "Because I don't like wasting anyone's time."

"Well if you're asking me if I want to marry you at some future date, how can I say yes or no? It'll depend on how I feel then. If I knew how I'd feel then I'd say so, but I don't."

"Okay, I won't pressure you."

She pointed her hands on her hips. "Good, because I don't like being pressured."

They both stared at each other for a moment. Joy hoped that would be the end of this topic and they could go back to being how they were. Then, Isaac walked away leaving her standing there. This time, she made no attempt to stop him. She had no patience for his sulky attitude. What she did regret was forgetting to buy her take-out coffee.

CHAPTER 14

*A*fter a week of Florence seeing Ezekiel nearly every day, the time came for him to leave. She'd gotten to know him as the strong quiet type. He saw humor in little things and was even-tempered. She saw nothing bad in him, and from what she knew of him, he seemed like a good choice for a husband.

They were alone on Florence's porch after he'd said goodbye to Wilma and the girls. It was just on dusk as they said their personal goodbyes. A car was coming to collect him from Ada and Samuel's house early the next morning.

"Florence, what I want to say to you is that I've enjoyed getting to know you."

"So have I. It's been really enjoyable."

He cleared his throat. "And there's something else I need to say."

She looked up at him. "And what's that?" She didn't want him to propose and she hoped that wasn't what he was about to do. If he did, she'd have to turn him down, but she didn't want to hurt his feelings and neither did she want to close any doors with him. Anxiousness caused her to bite down on the inside of her mouth.

"Would you write to me?"

That was it? Instead of heaving a large sigh, she contained it and nodded. "Of course, I'll write."

The serious look hadn't left his face. "I'm hoping there's something good in our future for the both of us."

"Me too. Time will tell."

His face softened when he laughed. "Not too much time, I hope. Might we see our friendship as something a little more while we write?"

"Jah. I thought that's what we were doing by agreeing to write to one another."

He nodded. "Good, I just wanted us both to be clear. Communication is very important in a relationship."

She wondered how often he'd write and what she'd write in return. Lots of things happened at the orchard, but most of it wasn't very interesting. He wouldn't want to know the latest dramas with the girls. Maybe she could tell him about the orchard and he could write to her about his farm.

Florence liked the way he got to the point about things. A

man like that would love her and cherish her. That was how she wanted to be treated by her husband and in return, she'd be a good wife.

She watched him get into the buggy. Once he'd picked up the reins, he moved them into one hand, and gave her a wave before he steered the horse and buggy down the long driveway.

Wilma hurried out to join her. "Well? Did he mention marriage?"

Florence put a hand over her mouth and giggled. *"Nee,* he didn't. But we're going to write to each other."

"He didn't discuss marriage at all?" *Mamm's* eyes opened wide.

"Nee, but I know he likes me. I think he knows me well enough to know that I'm not the kind of person who'd rush into something."

"Like Cherish?"

It wasn't only Cherish it was Honor, and possibly Joy as well, but Florence didn't want to say it. "I wasn't speaking about anybody. I think there could be something special between us. It's not a crazy kind of love at first sight or anything, it's more of a dependable kind of love."

"I agree, and he'd make a fine husband. Now, do you forgive me for allowing Honor to get married?"

"It's your choice. There's nothing to forgive. I wouldn't have allowed it, but that doesn't matter."

"When we have a moment alone, I'll tell you exactly why I allowed it and then you'll see there are at least two sides to a thing."

"Jah, there are. The right side and the wrong side."

Mamm shook her head. "What about the inside and the outside? We'll have that talk as soon as we're alone. Maybe when the girls are in bed."

"I can't wait to hear what you've got to say."

Mamm chuckled. "I'm so pleased you met Ezekiel. Ada's done well choosing men for you girls."

"She didn't choose Jonathon, or come to think of it, Isaac."

"Well, it's two out of four. And we didn't ask her to find anyone for Joy or Honor."

"Let's get in out of the cold," Florence suggested.

CHAPTER 15

*O*ver breakfast the next day, *Mamm* announced they needed Cherish back to help with the wedding preparations.

Honor groaned. *"Nee, Mamm.* You know how she thinks she's in love with Jonathon? How can I have her around at my wedding?"

"She's your *schweschder.* You can't leave her out of it."

"Nee! You can't do this to me."

Florence said, "How about she comes back just a day or two before. That way, everyone will be so busy it won't matter."

Honor shook her head. "I've got a better idea. How about she doesn't come back until the day, or even better, the day after."

"I'll arrange for her to come back two days before, and I

hope Dagmar can come with her. She'll have to find someone to look after her farm—I hope she's able to."

"Please, don't have a lot of attendants if you want me to sew," Florence told Honor.

"Nee, I'm only having Joy."

Everyone looked at Joy, who looked delighted.

"I knew you'd choose her," Favor said.

"She's the next closest in age, that's all. I'm not choosing favorites."

"That's fine by me."

"And, the men already have suits. Jonathon has the one he wore to Stephen's wedding and he's happy to wear that one again."

That was good news to Florence's ears. "You don't mind him not being in a new one?"

"Nee, it's a waste. It's money we can put toward our home when we get one."

Mamm and Florence exchanged smiles.

When Honor and Joy went to work at the markets, Florence sent Favor and Hope to clean the laundry room. She was anxious to hear what *Mamm* had to say about allowing Honor and Jonathon to marry. It sounded like Wilma had a story to tell. After Florence made two cups of coffee, she settled down with *Mamm* in the living room.

"Mamm, now we're alone ..."

"I can see you're still annoyed, Florence. Do you want to talk about it, or wait a bit?"

"Jah. Please begin. You said you'd tell me more when we were alone, and now we're alone." A wave of emotion came over Florence. It was awful having to discipline the girls when *Mamm* had the final say. "First Mercy and Stephen got married, which I suppose is fine because we all know they get on great. But now you've given Honor permission to marry Jonathon. Jonathon, of all people. And next, before we know what will happen, Joy will marry Isaac." She paused, drawing a breath.

"I know, but you like Isaac."

"That's not the issue. I'm worried that they're all getting married too young."

"They're marrying when they fall in love."

"But, are they old enough to know what love is?"

A small smile hinted around the edges of *Mamm's* lips. "Florence, let me tell you what I know. There was a woman I knew very well."

"Before you tell me a story, let me tell you one. There is a woman I know very well and she thought she was in love. After she married in haste, she had years of misery before *Gott* turned it around. I just don't think those years of misery were worth it. People say marriage takes work, but does it have to be that hard? And, perhaps it wouldn't be so much work if one chose one's husband more carefully. Those are some of my thoughts from what I've seen."

Mamm's eyebrows rose. "Florence, if you will listen to me, you'll see why I haven't put my foot down to stop your sisters from marrying."

"Go on."

"There was a woman who was very much in love with a man in the same community, but her parents thought she was too young."

"How young?"

"She was sixteen and the young man was eighteen. Their parents refused to allow them to marry. He went on to marry someone else years later."

"What happened to her?"

"Ah, that's a totally different story. Heartbroken that their parents wouldn't allow them to see one another, she left the community thinking that would make their parents agree to the marriage. It didn't happen. She got in with the wrong crowd, and became pregnant, or she might've already been pregnant before she left. That's my guess. Away from her friends and family and as an unmarried mother, she faced many struggles and her life was ruined."

"Who was it, *Mamm*?" Many scenarios ran through Florence's mind. She couldn't have been talking about herself, could she?

"I might as well tell you. To you, she'd be your step-Aunt Iris."

Florence tried to make sense of everything. She knew there wasn't an Iris on her father's side and she was sure her stepmother only had one *bruder, Onkel* Tom—and his wife's name was Ruth.

"I have a step-aunt, Aunt Iris? Is she your *schweschder?*"

"Jah. My younger *schweschder.* I haven't seen her for many years. She stopped by one day when I was pregnant with Mercy, and I told her she should leave. Something that I regret to this very day."

"You can't blame yourself. You thought you were doing the right thing."

"It doesn't matter what I thought. I've learned since then that closing my heart off to others doesn't help them. I mean, how could it?"

"Don't be so hard on yourself."

"I've never heard from her again. I think about her every day, hoping she'll find the courage to knock on my door."

Florence swallowed hard. That explained why *Mamm* was so soft on everyone. She'd been hard on her own sister and, as a result, lived with not knowing where Iris was or whether she was okay. And, *Mamm* had to wonder what had become of the *boppli.*

"I don't know what might happen, but do you see now why I am not standing in their way?"

Florence nodded. "I do. You're afraid if you stop them, they'll do something drastic."

"Well, also, imagine her heartbreak to learn that the man she loved and probably still does to this day is married to someone else."

Florence thought about that for a moment. "I wouldn't want any of my sisters to leave the community over a man."

"Honor very nearly did."

"I guess there are two different ways of looking at these things, aren't there? There is the story of my friend, and then there's Iris."

Mamm nodded. "And they're both true."

"And we're both trying to do the best we can for the girls."

"That's true. But I truly think at their ages they know their own minds."

"I'm sorry, *Mamm*, but I know when I was sixteen, I would have chosen a very different man compared to the one I'd choose today. Sixteen is not old enough."

"I must disagree with that."

"Denke for telling me about your sister. It's a sad story when you're not in love with the person you marry. You were in love with *Dat*, weren't you?"

"From as far back as I can remember." She giggled.

"Only after my *mamm* died though, right?"

"Of course."

Florence smiled. She'd only remembered her father with Wilma. From what she remembered, they'd been in love. They were always talking to each other, and they always agreed on everything.

"Our coffees have gone cold."

Florence giggled. "I'll make us more." She stood up, and leaned over and hugged Wilma. "I hope one day we'll find out what happened to your *schweschder.*"

"If *Gott* wills it, we will."

CHAPTER 16

*T*he weeks flew by and Florence was so busy organizing the household and the wedding, she hadn't had any time for herself. Now just two days remained before the wedding and it was time for Cherish to come home.

At five in the evening, Wilma excitedly yelled out, "She's here!"

Florence went to the kitchen window and looked out. Caramel, Cherish's dog, was out of the car first, and then Cherish stepped out looking none too happy. The expression on her face was exactly the same as the one she had worn when she left. Florence was immediately filled with dread. With so much left to do they didn't need any more complications.

The girls raced out to greet her and Florence was the last one. A tiny smile met Cherish's lips as her sisters hugged her in turn. Then Caramel charged at Florence pulling the leash out of Cherish's hand.

Florence bent down to pat him as he jumped up at her. "How have you been, boy?"

"It seems like you're more pleased to see Caramel than me."

She looked up to see Cherish right there. What she said was true, but Florence couldn't admit it.

"It's so nice to have you home," Florence stood up and hugged her, while Caramel ran onto the grass.

"I've got your bag, Cherish. I'll take it up to your room."

"Denke, Favor."

All the girls ran after Cherish to hear about her stay with Dagmar. That left Florence and *Mamm* standing at the bottom of the stairs.

"I know we haven't talked about this, but do you intend for Cherish to stay?" Florence asked.

"I've made no promises to her. Aunt Dagmar's pleased for her to go back to her. She's pleased for the companionship."

"So, you will send her back if she hasn't changed?"

"Jah, I don't want her to get into any kind of trouble."

Florence nodded as she recalled the conversation they'd had recently about Wilma's long-lost sister.

. . .

THAT NIGHT, WHEN EVERYONE WAS SEATED AROUND THE dinner table, Cherish began with the stories. "Aunt Dagmar has this tiny bird that she keeps in a cage. His name's Timmy. And all I hear all day is, *Timmy, Timmy, Timmy.* She's trying to teach him to talk."

The girls giggled.

"I can't tell you how annoying I find it. 'Timmy, Timmy,'" she tried to mimic Dagmar's voice and all the girls laughed louder.

"You should be grateful she's welcomed you with open arms," *Mamm* said.

"If she hadn't wanted me, where would you have sent me?"

"Somewhere really bad," Florence chipped in.

Cherish's eyes grew wide as she stared back at Florence. "It *is* really bad, Florence. Haven't you been listening to what I've been saying?"

"Nee, all I've heard is you being rude about a person who's been kind. It wouldn't hurt you at all to develop some patience and gratitude."

That kept everyone quiet for a few moments, until Cherish started once more. "I feel like a prisoner there. I don't have to go back there again, do I?"

"I told you, you can stay here as long as you behave."

Honor said, "And don't imagine that Jonathon likes you, please don't think that he does. He's marrying me. Anyway, you're far too young."

Cherish's face screwed up. "I didn't like him. Not like that," she insisted, but everyone knew she was making that up. Florence took a large drink of water, and when she put the glass down, Cherish said to her, "I hear you have a boyfriend."

Florence hadn't thought about Ezekiel as a boyfriend, but perhaps that's what he was. "Maybe I do."

"I heard he's a pig farmer. I bet he smells awful, a bit like a pig, or pig swill, or even pig manure."

Amongst a flurry of giggles, *Mamm* said, "Cherish, you shouldn't say such things."

"He does smell—he smells nice," Florence said, trying to make light of things.

Cherish's eyes danced with mischief. "Ah, so you've been close enough to smell him, have you?"

Mamm shook her head at her youngest. "No more, Cherish, or you'll be sent to your room."

Hope whispered in Cherish's ear, but it was loud enough for Florence to hear, "Don't say any more or they'll send you right back."

Cherish put her head down and then looked back up at *Mamm* and then Florence, as though summing them up. "I believe it," she muttered back.

"I hope everyone is ready to do a lot of work tomorrow," said *Mamm.* "We've got a big day ahead of us. All the ladies are coming to give the *haus* a going-through. Then the day after, we'll concentrate on the food."

"I was hoping to have a rest. Can't I have a rest?" Cherish whined. "I'm tired from all the traveling."

"You'll get a good sleep tonight and you'll be okay," *Mamm* said.

Cherish played with her food. "At least I know how to make baskets now."

"You should've brought some with you," Joy said.

"I'd like to know how to make baskets," Favor said.

"I can show everyone, if I get to stay here."

Favor leaned forward. "Was it really that bad?"

"I like Aunt Dagmar. I didn't at first, but then I got to like her. When she's not talking to Timmy, that is. The thing I don't like is, she lives out in the middle of nowhere and I feel like a prisoner. When I'm feeling sad, Dagmar starts talking to her stupid bird, trying to make him talk and that makes me feel worse."

Mamm smiled a little, and then coughed to cover it up. "What did Caramel think of the bird?"

"Nothing, nothing at all. He just ignored him." Cherish sighed. "I can't believe that there's just four of us left now."

Favor giggled. "Joy will be marrying Isaac next."

Florence suddenly realized they'd have to close down the stall at the farmers market. It wasn't practical for them to keep it going.

Joy shook her head when everyone stared at her. "That won't be happening. Not for years and years. Not for a couple of years, anyway. I'm in no rush, not like the rest of you."

"We aren't," Favor said. "I'm not."

"Neither am I," said Hope. "Maybe if there was someone I liked, I might be in a hurry, but there's no one for me."

"Well, if Florence can find someone, anyone can," said Cherish.

"*Denke,* Cherish." The comment was said to upset Florence, but she wasn't going to let what Cherish said bother her.

Mamm glared at her youngest. "It's not a very nice thing to say."

"Oh, I didn't mean it like that. I'm so sorry, Florence."

Florence smiled at her, figuring it was the best thing to do. "The ladies will be arriving early in the morning. We've got a busy day of cleaning ahead of us."

"The place is already clean, if you ask me," Favor said.

Mamm smiled. "It'll be cleaner than clean by the end of the day tomorrow."

CHAPTER 17

*T*he day after next—the day before the wedding —a crowd of women gathered at the house to cook, just as they had for cleaning the previous day. Even Jonathon came to see if he could be of any help. Wanting to keep Jonathon and Cherish far apart, Florence knew she'd have to keep him busy with jobs far away from Cherish.

For his first task, Florence asked him to go to the building that they operated as a shop, at the front of their property, to count the cakes that they'd stored there. Florence knew exactly what was there and how many of each, but Jonathon didn't know that.

When she went back to her own task, she noticed Cherish was leaving the cleaning task she'd been given, assisting with dishes for the cooks.

Florence quickly asked Favor to temporarily take over Cherish's task. When she stepped out onto the porch, she saw Cherish hurrying down the path that led to the shop. She was deliberately following Jonathon. This wasn't good.

Florence hurried to stop a disaster from happening. When she reached the door, she hovered to listen in.

"Hello, Jonathon."

"Hi, Cherish. It's a long time since I've seen you."

"I've just been visiting some relatives. I thought it was time I came home."

"Gut. In time to see your *schweschder* and I get married."

"Um, *jah* … about that."

Florence froze as she listened.

Cherish continued, "It's not too late to change your mind. Other people have done it. No one will think badly of you. People will respect you for making your own decision instead of being pushed into something."

"Now wait a minute. No one's pushing me into anything. I love her with all my heart, and we belong together. There's not one single solitary doubt in my mind. There's no reason to change anything."

"Really?" Cherish asked.

"Jah. What are you doing here anyway?"

"Florence sent me to count the cakes."

"You sure about that? It doesn't take two, and she asked

me to do that. I think you should go back. I'm not sure why we're even talking like this, and …"

Florence was pleased to hear his response and was just about to save him from Cherish, when she heard Cherish's next comment.

"But I'm in love with you, Jonathon."

Florence couldn't believe her ears. She waited to hear what Jonathon said.

"I'm sorry to hear that. That's something you should keep to yourself considering the situation."

"Nee, that's exactly why I must tell you; because you're making a big mistake."

"I'm not!"

Florence moved into the building, and Cherish turned around, shocked to see her. "I thought you were in the kitchen, Florence."

"I was, but we need you to keep cleaning up after the cooks as they work. Why did you leave?"

Cherish shook her head. "I'm talking to Jonathon."

Jonathon kept his head down. "You'd better go, Cherish."

Florence was livid that Cherish was so arrogant toward her. She grabbed her by the arm. "Back to the kitchen, now." Once they were out the door and halfway to the house, Florence said to her, "I heard what you said in there. I can't even believe my own ears. How could you say something like that? Are you trying to ruin your *schweschder's* life? What were you thinking?"

"I was doing nothing wrong. I just thought he might've been pushed into it and that's not fair."

Florence shook her head. "You're definitely going back to Aunt Dagmar's."

"Nee, Mamm won't allow it."

"If it's the last thing I do, I'll see that she's in full agreement with me."

"You wouldn't."

"Just watch me."

Once Cherish was back in the house, Florence took *Mamm* aside and told her what had happened. *Mamm* was greatly upset. "I think she'll have to go back."

Florence nodded. "I agree."

"I'll talk with her and make sure she behaves herself until she goes back to Dagmar's."

"And when will that be?" Florence asked, hoping it'd be soon.

"I'll talk with her now. I'll take her up to her room, so no one will hear us. I don't want Honor being upset over this. It's better she doesn't know, for now. Can you call Aunt Dagmar and make sure it's okay that she goes back there?"

"Sure. I'm happy to do it. Do you want me to call a driver and find one who can drive her there soon?"

Mamm nodded, and then sighed. "It's all too much for me, Florence. Please find someone who can drive her back there the next day after the wedding."

"Okay." From where they stood in the living room, Florence looked at all the workers in the kitchen. "I'll stay here until you talk with her. One of us should stay. When you come back, I'll go to the barn and make some calls."

"*Denke*, Florence."

EARLY THAT AFTERNOON, FLORENCE WALKED OUT OF THE barn ready to deliver the news to *Mamm* that a driver would be arriving at nine the morning after the wedding. That would mean Cherish would miss the big clean-up day after the celebrations, but Florence was certain her youngest half-sister wouldn't have made much of a contribution to that anyway. Dagmar was pleased with the news that Cherish would return.

While walking up the porch steps that led to the house, Florence spied a bundle of letters left on a chair. She picked up the half dozen letters and leafed through them for Ezekiel's familiar handwriting. Then she spotted it.

Florence was distressed to get a letter from him so close to the wedding. In her heart, she knew what that meant.

She sat on the porch chair, and then, with the other letters in her lap, she ripped open the envelope.

In his letter, Ezekiel explained his mother wasn't well and he wouldn't be attending the wedding. Dropping the letter into her lap, she looked out over the orchard. She'd been counting the days until she would see him, so they could continue their courtship. Even though she was against rushing into a relationship, neither did she want it to drag out for an eternity.

When would something ever go right for her?

There was no time to feel sorry for herself. Not with the wedding tomorrow. She picked herself up and fixed a smile on her face before she headed back into the house.

CHAPTER 18

*J*oy was excited to be participating in her sister's wedding, wearing the exact color medium-blue dress as Honor. As she sat behind Honor, who was standing in front of the bishop with Jonathon, it almost felt like her own wedding in a way. Especially with Isaac there looking so handsome in the dark suit that his older sister, Christina, had made him.

While the bishop gave his talk, she couldn't help looking over at Isaac. Each time she glanced at him, he smiled even wider. And then she noticed someone else's eyes upon her. It was Jonathon's younger brother, Luke, who was sitting behind Jonathon as his wedding attendant.

When their eyes met, he beamed her a smile and she turned away. Now she couldn't look at Isaac because Luke might think she was looking at him. So, she concentrated on the bishop's words as he spoke on the topic of *Gott's* plan for marriage.

．　．　．

HONOR GLANCED AT HER HUSBAND-TO-BE AS THEY STOOD
in front of the bishop in the family's living room. Just as it
had been for Mercy's wedding, all the furniture in the
house had been exchanged for wooden benches. Now
every one of those benches was full, leaving people to
stand on the sides of the room.

It felt good that so many people had come to see them get
married. And that no one had said anything about her
getting married so young. People seemed to like the idea
she and her older sister would be married to brothers.
Jonathon had even teased his young brother, Luke, that
he'd have to marry Joy. Honor knew that was very
unlikely because Joy only had eyes for her half-brother's
wife's brother. It was confusing, but many relationships
within the community were like that.

This marriage was what Honor and Jonathon had wanted
more than anything, and against all odds Jonathon had
made it happen. He convinced her mother that the timing
was right. With all that they'd been through together,
Honor knew he was the perfect man for her. They'd also
be moving close to Mercy. She glanced over her shoulder
to look at Mercy, and after they exchanged smiles, she
saw Florence staring at her disapprovingly. Quickly, she
faced the front. In time, Florence would learn that
Jonathon was a good man, and when she did, she might
even apologize for ever doubting him.

Once they were finally pronounced married, it was time

for the festivities. Everyone moved from the house into the annex that covered the area between the house and the barn.

THROUGHOUT THE CEREMONY, JOY HAD KEPT A CLOSE EYE on Isaac. When he didn't gravitate to her when the ceremony was over, she walked over to him. He saw her coming and then he deliberately moved away. Joy had no idea what had gotten into him. When she finally caught up with him, she saw from his face that he was upset.

"Is everything okay?"

He pressed his lips together. *"Nee."*

"What's wrong?"

"I saw you looking at someone else just now."

Joy laughed. "Don't be silly. I was looking at you."

"Not all the time."

Joy stared at him. Was he joking? When there was no hint of a smile on his face, she knew he wasn't. Being a no nonsense kind of a person, she wasn't in the mood for drama. Not on such a special day for her sister. "Find me when you get over the mood you're in." She turned and walked away from him. He must've been talking about when she had noticed Luke staring at her. Isaac was being immature and she wasn't going to be drawn into his silliness. Pushing him out of her mind, she walked amongst the crowd determined to enjoy herself and help the many guests enjoy themselves.

MEANWHILE, FLORENCE WAS WORKING IN THE KITCHEN supervising the ladies who were helping with food for the three hundred or so guests. Florence wasn't bothered by the huge task on her shoulders. She helped out so often at weddings. Years ago, her father had set their kitchen up with two large ovens and there was loads of countertop space for working.

Once the first course of the food had gone out, Florence was able to slow her pace. Yet, her mind never stopped working—never stopped thinking about the orchard and her family's finances. Their savings had taken a hit with Honor's wedding coming so close behind Mercy's. *Mamm* hadn't taken that into consideration when she'd allowed them to marry now rather than having them wait for a year.

With Cherish going back to Aunt Dagmar's, and the two oldest half-sisters now married, that only left five of them. As much as the money coming in from the farmers markets was a great help, she didn't see that they could continue that especially with the harvest approaching. Between the orchard and their shop, that was probably all they could manage. She made a mental note to cancel their stall at the farmers market.

A flushed-faced Christina hurried into the kitchen. "Florence, what's going on between Joy and Isaac?"

"I'm not sure I know what you mean."

"It seems they had a tiff. He barely talks to me and he keeps looking at Joy. She seems to be ignoring him."

"I'm sure they can work things out between themselves. In the meantime, can you take these napkins out and put them on the table?"

"Don't you care?"

"I'm too busy to even think about it now, Christina."

Florence held out the white napkins toward Christina. Christina snatched them from her. "You're the same as the rest of your family. Only thinking about yourself." She stomped away leaving Florence shocked. Her life was consumed with looking after others.

Ada was one of the ladies working in the kitchen and she'd overheard what Christina had said. "Don't worry about her, Florence."

"I don't know what I did to upset her."

"She's very highly strung." Ada shook her head. "Two years married and no *kinner.*"

"Is that what's upsetting her?"

"Jah. Mercy or even Honor might give birth before her. That's what she'd be thinking."

"Hmm, they both seem like *bopplis* themselves. Do you think that's really what's upsetting Christina?"

"I can't see what else it could be."

As far as Florence remembered, Christina had always been standoffish towards her family. Maybe one of them had done something to offend her. When two ladies walked in with stacks of dirty dishes, Florence's attention was back on the job.

JOY HAD BEEN SUCCESSFUL IN AVOIDING LUKE WILKES. Every time she looked over at Isaac, he avoided eye contact. Just as she was considering walking over to talk with Isaac to sort things out, someone tapped her on her shoulder. She turned around to see Christina, Isaac's sister.

"What's going on with you two?" Christina asked.

"Me and your *bruder?*"

"Jah,"

"Just a small misunderstanding. It's okay. I'm just giving him a bit of time to work a few things out."

"Don't you know he's leaving?"

It couldn't be true. "What?"

"Jah, he's leaving and I'm not talking about him leaving the wedding. He will be leaving. He was only staying here for you."

"I didn't know."

"Couldn't you figure that out? Now we've lost him working in the store just like we lost Jonathon. You girls have got a lot to answer for. That's another worker we've lost from our store because of you girls."

Even though she was sad about Isaac leaving, she wasn't going to let an opportunity go by. "I could work for you."

"Denke, but no thanks. I don't think you'd be reliable enough to work six days a week and do all the heavy lifting needed."

"I am reliable. Ask anyone, and I do heavy lifting at home. You'd be surprised how strong I am. I lift all the bags of horse feed."

"Your *mudder* and Florence need you at home, at the market stall, and to do the cooking and what not."

"Okay." Joy shrugged her shoulders. "At least I offered to help out."

"Hmm. I'm not sure if it was a genuine offer or not."

Joy could now see the side of Christina that her sisters so often talked about. She wasn't very pleasant. She was always nice to Honor, and even more so since Jonathon had stayed with them. "I hope you find someone for the store." She wasn't going to beg Isaac to stay if he wanted to go.

"There's a shortage of jobs, so it won't take long for us to find someone, but Isaac is my *bruder,* so I'm not happy. He wasn't just a worker."

"I know that's upsetting for you, but it's not my fault. If you want him to stay, just ask him."

"You should be the one asking him. He might stay if he knows you want him to. Aren't you the least concerned that he's leaving?"

"I am, but there's not much I can do if he wants to go."

Christina looked over her shoulder at Isaac and then looked back at Joy. "Do what you want. You girls always do. Wilma hasn't disciplined any one of you." Christina walked away from her.

Joy wasn't going to leave things at that. She hurried after Christina to have her say. "She doesn't need to discipline us if we never do anything wrong."

Christina's eyes blazed. "You do plenty wrong."

Joy knew she couldn't protest, not with both Honor and Cherish having tried to run away. "Well, everyone does wrong things, but I think it's a bit harsh to say that we're not disciplined. You're being disrespectful to my *mudder.*"

"That's a matter of opinion."

"I'll talk to Isaac." She was going to do that anyway.

"Denke, that's all I was asking."

When Christina walked away, Joy headed in the direction she'd last seen Isaac. When she got there, she saw him sitting down by himself eating a piece of cake. She walked up and sat beside him. "Why are you sitting down by yourself?"

"I don't know these people very well."

"You know them well enough, don't you?"

"Nee."

"When I first met you, you didn't seem shy at all. You were bold and led the conversations and now you're sitting here quietly filling your face with food."

"I like food, can't you tell?" He pushed a huge piece of cake into his mouth.

"It seems you like cake. I can tell that much." Scriptures ran through her mind, as they so often did, and she wondered if he had a problem with gluttony. *For the drunkard and the glutton shall come to poverty: and drowsiness shall clothe a man with rags.* But, who was she to judge someone? It did make her cautious about him. It wasn't his size that was a problem, though, it was his bad attitude.

When he finished his mouthful, he said, "I made the decision I'm going back home."

"I don't want you to go. I want you to stay."

Without answering her, he pushed the last piece of cake into his mouth and with his finger, gathered the last of the frosting and popped that into his mouth also.

"My, you're really enjoying that cake."

"I know exactly what you mean by that. You can have any man you want and you don't want someone like me. I'm overweight. I know it's a problem, but the more I think about it the more I eat."

"Forget about it, then. Problem solved."

"It's not so easy."

"You're not fat at all. I like the way you look. You have a large frame and there's nothing wrong with that."

"I appreciate you trying to be nice, but there's no point anymore." With his plate in his hand, he rose to his feet, and then she watched him walk back to one of the food tables. At that point, she decided he was in a strange mood and nothing she could say would bring him around. With Honor leaving early tomorrow morning, she decided to spend the rest of the day as close to her as she possibly could.

HONOR LEFT WITH JONATHON THE VERY NEXT DAY. CHERISH was picked up at nine that same morning for the return trip to Aunt Dagmar's, and one week after that, Isaac was gone. Isaac and Joy had not spoken once after the wedding.

The Baker household was quiet.

IN TRYING TO MAKE THINGS WORK WITH EZEKIEL, Florence had deliberately kept herself away from Carter,.

but that didn't stop the aching in her heart. She longed to be loved by one special person and for now, Ezekiel was falling way short of the mark.

When the sun was low in the sky, loneliness and frustration led her through the orchard and toward Carter's house. All she intended to do was catch a glimpse of him. When the house came into view, she saw his car there but there was no sign of him.

Florence walked close to the fence. Maybe she should knock on his door and just see him one last time? Where was the harm in that?

Before she lost her sudden courage, she slipped through the five-strand wire fence. Halfway to his house, she stopped still as doubts crept into her mind.

He's an outsider, she reminded herself. Ezekiel Troyer was the kind of man she should marry. Ezekiel was the sensible choice, but she'd come this far.

As she stared through one of his windows, she knew she had to close the door of her heart once and for all. It would be hard, but then she brought to mind the suffering of her forefathers and what they'd endured in the name of God. Just staying away from a man was no comparison. She wasn't being tortured or killed. She sighed, summoned the courage, and walked away from his house.

Getting to know Ezekiel would keep her mind busy and put a stop to her thinking about Carter.

"Hey."

Her heart raced when she recognised his voice. She turned around but she couldn't see him.

"Over here," the voice said. She followed the sound and saw him coming toward the fence from the orchard. "It seems we both had the same idea. I was looking for you."

She hurried over to him, horrified. "You didn't go to the house?" What would her stepmother think if an *Englischer* knocked on the door looking for her? Besides that, it would be a dreadful example to her half-sisters. They met as they always seemed to, at the fence.

"I was looking for you." He gave her a smile, flashing his white teeth. His cheeks were slightly pink blending nicely with the hue of his maroon knitted scarf that hung casually around his neck.

He looked so good. Coming to see him was a huge mistake. They needed more than a wire fence between them. "Look, this is your side of the fence and that is my side. Stay on your own side and everything will be fine." She pulled up one of the wire strands to slip through and he tried to help her. "I can do it," she snapped.

He frowned. Now they were both on her side of the fence. "Why the anger?" he asked.

"I can't keep talking to you like this—all friendly like." Her whole body trembled.

He grinned. "Why?"

"I just can't."

"You can't be friends with someone of a different faith? Or someone who has no faith at all?"

"No, I mean, that's right."

He rubbed the back of his neck. "I see Amish people talking to non-Amish people all the time."

"Talking yes, but we're not close."

It annoyed her that she'd never found out more about him, but that might've been the attraction. If she knew everything about him maybe he wouldn't seem so interesting. She had to know more, and then she'd finally have the courage to forget him.

He carefully ran his fingers along the top row of barbed wire. "I saw you with a man the other day. You both looked happy."

"We're just friends." That was her chance. She could've pretended things were serious between her and Ezekiel. Now was also her chance to know about that woman. "I've seen a woman here a few times while I've been on my afternoon walks."

"She's just a friend."

"You're only saying that because I said the man was just a friend."

"No." He shook his head. "She's truly just a friend."

"I thought you didn't need friends."

"More of an acquaintance." He laughed. "It's not like that. I know what you're thinking."

"I'm not thinking anything."

"Anyway, all that aside, I'm glad he's only a friend of yours."

"Why's that?" She knew she should walk away, but she couldn't. Besides, he'd been so good to her when Honor had run off with Jonathon. He'd driven through the night and that was after spending the whole day driving around locally looking for her.

"He doesn't suit you at all." He wagged a finger at her. "You're scared of getting to like me too much, aren't you?"

"No!" Her nervous fingers straightened her *kapp.* "Of course not! I would never—"

He smirked. "But you've thought about it."

She shook her head and annoyance took over before she got a chance to ask more questions. "It's best that you stay on your side of the fence and I'll stay on mine."

"Is that what you want?"

"Yes."

"Come on. I'm sorry if I've upset you."

She walked away leaving him standing there. The only way she could finally end this was to do it this way. If they parted amicably, it would leave the door open.

"Florence."

She ignored him.

"I'll be here when you've gotten over whatever's bugging you," he called after her.

Just put one foot after the other.

Once she was far enough away among the safety of her apple trees, she slowed her pace. As she walked, she looked up through the high branches at the gray sky above. In her youth, she'd expected to grow up and marry. It seemed a simple thing.

It was irritating that love was happening so easily for her sisters. It wasn't that she was envious, it just left her with so many unanswered questions.

If she could fall in love with Ezekiel Troyer, her life would be wonderful. To have *kinner* of her own would be a dream come true. She quickened her pace, determined to write another letter to Ezekiel before the evening meal.

CHAPTER 19

*I*t was months after Honor and Jonathon's wedding and everything had returned to normal—a new version of normal—in the Baker household. Another apple harvest had come and gone—this time, without three of Florence's half-sisters. They no longer had the stall at the farmers markets and concentrated their efforts on their shop down by the road. Florence had kept her word and sent regular letters to Ezekiel Troyer, but his letters were fewer than what she would've liked. It was hard to develop a meaningful relationship without regular contact. In his letters, he'd asked more than once if she'd come to see him. It would be difficult to leave the orchard, but Florence was starting to realize she had to make some effort.

Her best friend Liza now had her second baby—another boy—a brother for Malachi.

It was the best moment in Florence's life to witness a baby coming into the world. First off in the labor, came Liza's suffering leaving Florence utterly helpless, not knowing what to do other than look on. Nothing gave Liza comfort until the hours of those first-stage contractions passed. When the urge came to Liza to bear down, it wasn't long before the baby boy slithered out. Everyone was in tears. Florence hadn't been prepared for the miracle to be so impactful. It was a moment she'd remember for ever, and was grateful her very best friend had shared that special moment with her. It was a true gift. She hoped Liza would be at her own baby's birth—one day.

Florence had some serious catching up to do with Liza, who was two children and one husband ahead of her. But for that to happen, she needed her own man. That was another reason to make the effort to visit Ezekiel.

It was late one night when she was sewing with *Mamm* that she raised the subject of Cherish. If she'd learned her lesson, there would be another pair of hands to fill in for her when she visited Ezekiel. "When do you think would be a good time for Cherish to come home?"

Mamm jerked her head up from her sewing. "I was thinking about her just now! It's like you heard my thoughts. She hasn't been writing those pleading letters for a while now, and that's making me nervous."

"*Jah,* I noticed her letters had stopped."

"Why don't you call Dagmar and find out how Cherish's been doing?"

"We can both call her tomorrow and say happy birthday

to Cherish. That is, if they hear the phone in the barn from the *haus*."

"That's right. It'll be her birthday. How could I have lost track of that? I guess because she's not here ..."

"I know Cherish will be upset that she won't make it back for Joy's birthday and for hers." Joy's birthday was the day after Cherish's. They were one day off being born exactly three years apart.

"She should've thought of that before she started chasing someone far too old for her."

Florence nodded in agreement as the words brought the memories back. As they sat quietly by the toasty crackling fire, her thoughts turned to Carter. She hadn't seen him for months. He still lived there. She knew that because she often saw his car there.

"What are you thinking about with that faraway look in your eyes?"

"Nothing. Well, I was thinking how peaceful it is tonight."

"I wonder if it will ever be like that again once Cherish returns?"

Florence giggled. "Let's enjoy it while we can, shall we?"

Mamm smiled and nodded.

THEY CALLED AUNT DAGMAR THE NEXT MORNING, BUT there was no answer. It wasn't until the night-time that they spoke to Cherish. Nothing was discussed about when she'd be allowed home. Dagmar had arranged a special birthday dinner and Cherish was only interested in getting back to the guests.

The whole day Florence had waited anxiously for the mail to be delivered. When it finally came, there was only one letter in the box. It had come from one of Favor's many pen pals. There was nothing from Ezekiel.

ON NOVEMBER 5, THE MORNING OF JOY'S SEVENTEENTH birthday, Joy stayed in bed tossing and turning. Every night was the same. She couldn't sleep for thinking about Isaac and wondering if they'd ever be back to how they once were. He'd been so easy to get along with, and then he had changed.

In her mind, she'd analyzed every conversation, every glance, every action, wondering what had upset him. She must've done something. She'd written to him and even asked his sister, Christina, many times how he was. All Christina did was give a little smile and then change the subject. And she didn't want to get her half-brother Mark involved. He would be uncomfortable talking about the matter. She tried not to worry about it and to leave it in *Gott's* hands, but it wasn't as easy as she thought. Every time she managed to push it out of her head, it was there again five minutes later.

Luke Wilkes, her sort-of brother-in-law hadn't helped

matters with Isaac. Isaac was jealous and for no good reason. She couldn't help it if Luke had shown her attention at Honor and Jonathon's wedding. His interest was certainly not returned. He was too immature, not serious about much of anything.

Maybe everyone was right and she would be like Dagmar, and remain a spinster forever. Passed by, overlooked, and forgotten about. At least she'd have memories of Isaac and the times they once shared. If only he'd stayed the confident, carefree man she'd first met.

Then it occurred to her that he might have a girlfriend by now. Her stomach churned. Surely, she would've heard about it if he'd gotten married.

There was nothing she could do but trust *Gott* that He had a plan for her life. For all her preaching at others over the years, she was failing dreadfully in the trusting department. Why was such a simple thing as trusting so hard to do?

JOY HAD TAKEN OVER MERCY'S OLD BEDROOM AND SHE JUST happened to look out the window to see Isaac getting out of Christina and Mark's buggy. She could barely believe her eyes.

He's back!

Her heart felt like it had stopped for a moment. She put a hand to her chest and then sat down, as though frozen.

"If he's here that means he doesn't have a girlfriend and he's not married. Or is he coming to tell me he is getting married?"

Surely not on my birthday.

No, he was there to make up for lost time. To make amends. Maybe to apologize because he realized she had done nothing wrong.

She already had on her best dress for her birthday and one of Christina's specially sewn *kapps.*

She blew out a deep breath and walked down the steps in just enough time to hear Christina say, "We had an unexpected visitor today so we thought we'd bring him along. I hope that's okay."

"Isaac, it's nice to see you again," *Mamm* said.

She paused on the steps and he looked up at her and then everyone else faded into the background. "Joy," he said as he stood there staring.

"Hello, Isaac." She continued walking down the steps feeling like she was floating.

"Happy birthday,"

"Denke. You are staying for dinner, aren't you?"

He nodded. "That's why I've come." He handed her a slip of paper.

"What's this?"

"Read it." She slowly opened it and read it.

I'M SORRY FOR WHAT I'VE DONE AND I'M SORRY FOR THE TIME that we've been apart.

HER HEART MELTED. IN ONE MOMENT, ALL THE HEARTACHE was gone. She folded the note over. "I'm sorry too."

"Why don't we make a new start of things?" He grinned.

She stared at him. Why was he back now all of a sudden? Had he been dating another girl and she'd rejected him? That would explain Christina's behavior and the way she always avoided answering questions about him.

"What do you say?"

She realized she hadn't answered. "*Jah*, a fresh start."

"I can't change my weight. For starters, I've got big bones."

"Why would you want to change your weight?"

"For you."

"*Nee.* I l… like you just the way you are." She nearly said the word *love,* but wasn't prepared to say that word unless he said it first. She'd been disappointed by him once and didn't want a repeat.

"I've been miserable for months. Just ask my whole family."

She was pleased to hear it. "Are you feeling better now?"

When Isaac smiled at her, she knew everything would be okay.

"I'm fine. I just feel funny sometimes because I'm so overweight."

"You're not overweight, you're just perfect. I keep saying the same thing. Please, let's stop talking about it."

"I'm sorry for before."

"That's fine, forgiven, and there's no need to ever feel anything like that. To me, you're perfect just the way you are."

"I don't know about that, but thanks for saying so."

"Good. Now we can forget about all that and go back to how things were."

"Sure. I came to the conclusion it was all in my head." He held out his hand and she put her hand in his. "You'll have to catch me up with what you've been doing."

"I will, and it'll take all of five minutes because I've just been doing the same old thing over and over again."

Joy was relieved he was back. If he had been dating another girl, he wouldn't have said what he just had. Even though they'd never made promises to one another, it would've been awful if she had lost him. She couldn't imagine herself with anyone else and she wanted him to feel that way too.

"I remember when I reached seventeen. Do you feel any older?"

"Not a bit."

They walked into the dining room where they found everyone had gathered. Ada and Samuel, *Mamm's* close friends were there. They came to all the birthday dinners and family celebrations.

FLORENCE WAS FEARFUL NOW THAT ISAAC WAS BACK. Would Joy think she could also get married at seventeen just because her older sister had?

Half of her was worried, the other half really liked Isaac. And he was Christina's brother, and they'd known him for a long time. It was nice how he had surprised Joy by coming to her birthday dinner.

Once dinner was over and everyone was in the living room, Ada and Florence went into the kitchen to make coffee.

"Now come here and talk to your Aunt Ada."

Florence laughed. She wasn't her aunt, but her stepmother and Ada were so close she felt like her aunt. "All right. I'll just light the stove." When she had put the kettle to heat on the gas flame she sat down next to Ada.

"I think we should have a talk about something."

"What is it?"

"It's about Ezekiel."

"He's alright isn't he?"

"He's fine. But … I asked him how things were going with both of you and he said you were still writing."

"Jah, we are."

"I haven't finished yet."

"Oh, I'm sorry. Go on."

"He said he has invited you to the farm several times and you find a reason why you can't go."

"And the reasons are real. I'm not making them up. I'm thinking of going soon. Really I am."

"You should. He's a good man and you don't want to let him get away."

I know."

"Wilma tells me our Cherish might be coming back."

Florence nodded. "We have talked about that."

"That will give you more free time."

"No, it won't because I will have to keep an eye on her. Nothing ever runs smoothly when she's around. I first thought it would be good to get her back before I go away, but I just don't know."

"That's only because everyone is reliant on you now. If you didn't check on everything people would check on themselves." She leaned closer and whispered, "even Wilma has become too reliant on you. Once you're gone, they'll realize exactly how much you do."

"I will go to visit him, Ada. *Denke* for prompting me. I think I just needed a little push."

Ada put her arm around Florence's shoulder. "You deserve a lot of happiness, Florence. Your father and your mother would be pleased to see how lovely you've grown up to be."

She stared at Ada. Her mother was so rarely mentioned by anyone. "Were you close with my *mudder?*"

Right at that moment, the kettle boiled and Wilma walked into the room. "Florence, why don't you talk to our guests while I help Ada in here."

"Nee, Mamm. That's fine."

"I insist."

"Okay." Florence left the kitchen and headed to the living room. It felt strange having someone else do the work in the kitchen. The only seat left was one next to Christina, so she sat down next to her. There was no reason why they couldn't get along together and Florence was determined to make a special effort. Talking to Christina would also take her mind off what happened in the kitchen just now. Obviously, *Mamm* had overheard them talking about her birthmother. Was she jealous of even the memory of *Dat's* first wife?

CHAPTER 20

Two days later, Florence had booked into a bed-and-breakfast, for one week in mid-December, close to Ezekiel's farm. She knew he'd complain and insist on her staying at the house. She intended to refuse since his mother hadn't been well and she didn't want to put any undue stress on the poor woman. In a letter, she sent him all the details and all the dates.

Two weeks later she had a reply. She took it into the living room to read, unable to keep the smile from her face as she ripped open the envelope, but that smile fled from her face when she read what he had written. She looked it over again, hoping she'd somehow read it wrong.

DEAR FLORENCE,

I'm sorry to say that my mother has had a small relapse. It

wasn't helped by one of my brothers suddenly moving away leaving me busier than ever. I was hoping you might be able to delay your visit.

I have made some attempt over these past months to have someone look after the farm so I can come to see you. Each time, something gets in the way.

Perhaps this is God's way of telling us something?

I still think about my visit to you and I have pleasant memories of you, your family, and your apple orchard.

Look after yourself Florence.

Yours faithfully,

Ezekiel Troyer.

It was just so short. It was a goodbye letter. There was no doubt about it.

"What's that you've got?" Wilma walked into the room with a basket of clean clothes that needed to be ironed. Florence was so upset she couldn't speak. All she could do was pick up the letter and extend it toward her stepmother.

Mamm put the basket of clothes down on the couch and took hold of the letter.

Once she was finished reading it, she looked at Florence. "Are you going to cancel your vacation?"

"I have to. I can't really go there now after that letter. Do you think he was saying goodbye?"

Wilma licked her lips and looked down at the letter. "It seems he thinks everything is against you two being together. It's hard with you both living so far apart."

Florence felt she would burst into tears. In faith, she'd turned her back on the *Englischer* from next door and put all her energies into the possibility that she might one day be Mrs. Ezekiel Troyer.

The problem was, she wasn't good enough for him to make the required effort.

She felt fat, ugly, old, tired, and used up. No wonder no one loved her.

All she wanted was to be happy and feel loved. Was that too much to ask?

Mamm handed her back the letter. Florence took it and tossed it into the fire. Her quick actions shocked even herself. She could feel that Wilma was also amazed.

Wilma then picked up the basketful of clothes and continued on her way to the kitchen, where the clothes were normally ironed.

Then Florence heard her call out, "Don't forget to cancel the booking at the bed-and-breakfast."

"I'll remember." Florence sniffed back her tears. She's been so looking forward to meeting Ezekiel's family, helping his mother around her house, and looking around the pig farm. Now that door was firmly closed. No, it had been slammed in her face. Her letters had outnumbered his by three to one. There was no excuse for that because she was just as busy, or even more so. Yet, she had continued to convince herself that all was okay. He had certainly given her the impression that he was interested before he left and she had no idea why he so suddenly lost interest.

IT WAS TIMES LIKE THESE SHE NEEDED THE COMFORT THAT only a mother could give. She knew she'd been loved by her birth mother. If she had something tangible, like a pillow or a blanket that used to be hers, she could put it on her bed at night, and feel her close.

She remembered the attic where her mother's and father's things were stored. While her stepmother was busy in the kitchen, and her sisters were out with friends, she opened the small door of the attic and climbed up the stairs.

It was semi-dark and smelled so musty. The only light shone from a small window in the roof.

The place was lined with boxes, all piled one on top of the other. She and Earl were the ones who'd placed their father's belongings up here and she remembered where those had been placed. The rest of the boxes must've belonged to her mother.

The first box she opened was full of letters. Curiosity got

the better of her when she saw an envelope with her name on the front, and two other envelopes named for each of her brothers.

When she opened *her* letter, she looked at the date. It was dated a month before her mother had died. She stood up and taking the letter with her, she walked closer to the window so she could read it more easily.

My dearest Florence,

If you're reading this letter that means I'm no longer around. I've asked your father to give you this letter when you're an adult, the same as the letters I have for Mark and Earl.

Life is so uncertain.

I've learned nothing is forever. I want to be there always, guiding you and your brothers, whispering in your ears. If I can't be there, pay attention to my following words and keep them in your heart.

Always be kind to others.

Try to see the other person's point of view. It's just as valid as your own.

You must follow your heart rather than your head sometimes.

Don't make my mistakes.

No matter where I am, I will always love you, your father and your brothers.

Always be there for your family.

Your loving *Mamm*

HER MISTAKES. WHAT WERE HER MISTAKES?

She looked at those many letters. Perhaps in that box lay the answer?

Folding the letter carefully, she set it on the windowsill to collect later and sat down on the floor in front of the box to sort through the letters. After fifteen minutes of skimming through all the correspondence, she saw there was nothing helpful. At the bottom of the box she found a key. She held it up in the half-light—it was a small key, not big enough to open a door. Then her eyes traveled to a small wooden box wedged between the cardboard boxes. She pulled it out, admiring the beauty of woodgrain and workmanship as she turned it to find the lock, and then tried the key. It opened and there were more letters. Perhaps these were personal letters between her parents when they had been courting.

When she picked up the first envelope she turned it over and saw the last name of Braithwaite. She was sure her eyes were playing tricks on her, so she took it over to the light. Sure enough, the last name was Braithwaite and the first name was Gerald.

With her heart pounding in her head, she took out the single-page yellowed letter. Scanning the words, she saw it was a heartfelt plea. The man was pleading with her to come away with him and to leave the community. Florence dropped the letter and her hands covered her mouth. Her own mother must've been in love with someone before she married *Dat*.

She clutched her throat. Braithwaite. That was Carter's last name and it wasn't a common one, as far as she knew.

Then she recalled that Carter had once specifically asked her about her mother. What did it all mean?

She peered out the small attic window. On her tiptoes, she could just make out the roof of Carter's house peeping above the trees. Could she, or should she ask him questions?

Follow your heart. Don't make the same mistake as me. The words rang in Florence's head and that was all she needed. Despite the other voices in her head that told her not to do anything in haste, she put everything back where it had been, and climbed down the stairs She found Wilma in the kitchen.

"I'm going for a walk." Before Wilma could respond, Florence had grabbed her shawl and was out the door heading to Carter's house as she swirled it around her shoulders.

She had been so horrible to him last time and he had done nothing to deserve it.

Was it possible for people from two different worlds to come together and find some common ground? She couldn't see herself in his world, and she knew he wouldn't fit into hers, but her mother's letter must've meant something. Didn't it?

She knew there was a scripture in the Bible that said anything was possible with God. Joy would know the exact words and exactly where in the Bible it was.

This morning she'd felt sadness, but now all she had in her heart was the happiness of many possibilities. Perhaps it was possible, while putting God first, to follow your heart and find your dreams.

She slid between the wires of the fence, ever mindful of the barbs, and then walked quickly to Carter's door before she changed her mind. She knocked on the door and was pleased that he answered it when he did, before her courage left her.

"Florence." He looked her up and down as though he was taking it all in. "You came back."

"I never left."

"I haven't seen you for several months."

"That's an exaggeration." She inhaled quickly, then said, "I've come to say I'm sorry. I think we parted on bad terms. I'm here to say that I'm sorry for how I acted and the things I said."

"I don't remember who said what. I only know that after

it was said, you hurried away and wouldn't stop when I called you back. I waited and then went through the orchard looking for you, but couldn't find you."

"Did you?"

"Yes. After I got over the shock of being spoken to like that." He grinned.

"So, do you forgive me?"

"There's nothing to forgive. I'm pleased you're here now."

"I want to ask you a question."

"Fire away."

"You've asked me about my mother a couple of times."

"Yes, and you asked me about my family. What of it?"

This wasn't going to be easy. "This may sound totally crazy and maybe it is, but did you or anyone in your family know my birth mother?"

He stared at her blankly. "I'm not sure what you're asking."

There was no way around it—she had to tell him. "I was going through my mother's things today, something that I've never done before. Well, I made an attempt years ago, but it was a bit more upsetting than I could handle then, so I stopped. Anyway, I found some interesting things. There were letters from someone with the last name of Braithwaite. Those letters were addressed to my mother."

SAMANTHA PRICE

"Ah, now the penny drops. Is that the only reason you're here?"

She suddenly felt giddy and light-headed, but she couldn't stop asking or she might never again have the courage to ask. "No, I am here to apologize, but also to find out if there's any connection between someone with the last name of Braithwaite and my mother."

"There obviously was since you said they wrote her a letter. Are you asking me if there's anyone I know of in my family who wrote to your mother?"

"Yes. That's what I'm asking. His name was Gerald Braithwaite."

He blinked slowly, a few times, showing no recognition of that name. "What kind of letters were they?"

"I didn't read all of them but they appear to be love letters." When he smirked, she quickly added, "From before my mother married my father."

"That's interesting. Braithwaite is not an Amish name."

"That's right, I don't recall any Amish person having that name. Or anyone marrying into the Amish, but it's not impossible." Then it hit her like a bolt of lightning on a summer's day. Her mother had been in love with a non-Amish man. She turned her back on him and all that he represented to stay within the community and ended up marrying her father. That had to be the mistake her mother referred to since it followed the advice to follow her heart.

Joining the dots, that meant her mother regretted marrying her father. She'd always imagined her parents had an idyllic marriage and the perfect life. It wasn't so. The real love story never happened because her mother's heart belonged to Gerald Braithwaite.

Everything around her faded, and she collapsed into Carter's arms.

CHAPTER 21

When Florence opened her eyes, she was lying on Carter's couch, in his living room, and he was kneeling beside her.

She tried to sit up.

"Stay there." He held up his hand. "You fainted. I'll get you a glass of water."

Her heavy eyelids closed, and then he was back. He helped her sit up and plumped up some cushions behind her back. She brought the glass up to her lips and took a couple of sips.

"I'll take you to the hospital to get checked out."

"No. I'm fine." She wasn't really. She felt weird and drained of energy. Her fingers wrapped around the cool glass.

"People don't faint unless there's a problem. Has it happened before?"

"Only once. When I heard my father had died." She took a deep breath.

"What brought it on?"

She looked up at him standing there with his hands on his hips. "It was the shock of going through my mother's things. I'm sure of it. It brought a lot of things up from the past."

"Bad things?"

"Not really. It's hard to explain. I should go home." Leaning forward, she put the glass on the coffee table.

If she got away by herself, she could think things through. She stood up, took a step and then her foot caught on the edge of the rug and she fell toward him. His arms encircled her as she leaned into the hardness of his chest.

She looked up into his unusual colored eyes. They weren't brown or even a typical hazel; there were flecks of green and gold, and gray—light gray and charcoal, and ...

"You're beautiful, Florence."

She wanted to believe his words. She wanted him to kiss her, and just like that, his gaze traveled from her eyes to her mouth.

Florence's mother had given her the permission to follow her heart and, in that micro-second in time, that was what she wanted. She clung to him wanting him to kiss her and just before it happened, she moved her head. He pulled her into him instead, and she rested her head against his shoulder.

Suddenly, she couldn't let this madness continue. "I'm sorry. I tripped." She put her hands on his chest, pushing as she stepped back.

His hands moved to her shoulders and lingered as though he didn't want to let her go. "That's the stupid rug. I only just bought it yesterday. I'm sorry about that."

"It's okay. I have to go."

"Stay awhile."

"No. They'll come looking." It was a lie. There was no one who'd be looking for her, and the only place she wanted to be was here with him.

"Let me walk you home."

She shook her head, knowing there'd be too many questions from her family if they saw her with an *Englischer*.

"Partway, at least. I insist."

"Okay, if you insist."

"I do. I just said so." With a hand lightly on her arm, he guided her out of the house. "Are you warm enough?"

"Plenty." She glanced at his smiling face and adjusted her shawl. "I'm sorry about fainting."

He laughed. "You were determined to be in my arms one way or another today."

"I didn't do it deliberately. And your rug … I tripped on it."

"I'm not complaining, believe me."

While she was with him, she never wanted to leave. She never felt anything like this with Ezekiel. They reached the border of their two properties far too soon. "I'll be alright from here."

"No. I'll take you further."

"I'll be okay."

He pressed his lips together and shook his head. "Well, don't leave it so long next time. Will you come and see me tomorrow? Tomorrow morning? I'll be home all day."

"Those chess games on your computer sure must be interesting. Do you still do that all day?"

"Not all day. I do other things. I might even tell you one day, but you'll never know if you don't come back."

"I will."

Then there was a silent moment as their eyes said goodbye. Then he took a step closer, causing her heart to flutter like a butterfly just emerged from her chrysalis and finding her wings for the very first time. With his hand on the small of her back, he pulled her into him. Their bodies nearly touched as he lowered his head to hers. This time she stayed still. As soon as their lips touched, she pulled away.

"I have to go."

He released her. When she reached for one of the wires, he separated them so she could slip more easily through the fence. Once she was on the other side, she thanked him and bid him goodbye.

"Bye, Florence," he called after her as she hurried away into her orchard.

Florence made it to the first line of trees and looked back. He was out of sight, so she stopped and leaned on a tree. She felt different—everything did. As she looked above, she saw the sky was bluer, the white clouds fluffier, and she could even smell the crisp air.

Happiness flooded through her, her heart took wing, and she became fully alive.

A light had been shone into the darkness of her life.

Is this what it feels like to be loved and wanted?

Florence gulped and lowered herself to the cold ground beneath her and leaned back onto the friendly trunk of the apple tree.

The last thing she wanted to do was ruin this delightful giddy moment by being practical, but Carter wasn't from her world.

As much as she wanted to be close to him and learn everything about him, it was *verboten.*

She sighed loudly.

If only they'd had just one last kiss.

Just one.

That kiss would've lasted her a lifetime.

"Florence!"

She looked over at the sound of Carter's deep voice and saw him running toward her.

"Are you okay?"

"I am."

He crouched down beside her. "What are you doing on the ground like this?"

Here was her chance for just one kiss—a proper kiss.

The memory of which would last a lifetime.

What would the harm be in just one simple kiss?

She could be practical tomorrow, and in time, she'd marry someone suitable—a sensible man. Then she'd go on to have a sensible family with many sensible children. Or not ... Maybe she'd be like Aunt Dagmar, running the orchard as an unmarried businesswoman.

This kiss would be her one indulgence—something that would be hers and hers alone to remember when times got tough. She could close her eyes and remember her first kiss with the man her heart wanted.

If and only if, he wanted to kiss her again.

"I was just thinking." She held out her hands, and just as she knew he would, he stood and as he did he pulled her to her feet with him. Once they faced one another, they stared into each other's eyes.

Because she'd twice rejected him, she knew she had to make the first move.

She took a step to him and turned her face upward. He wasted no time in lowering his head until their lips met. The warm, gentle and love-filled kiss was everything she'd hoped it would be.

His lips were soft and loving—his arms, strong, manly, and reassuring.

In that moment, she felt loved like she'd never felt before.

"Oh, Florence." He hugged her to himself. "There are so many things you don't know about me."

It was dangerous to get too close and she hoped with that kiss that he hadn't taken it as something more than it was.

Summoning all her strength, she said, "I have to go."

"Don't!" He leaned down and kissed her forehead.

"There's always tomorrow."

"I'll be waiting. Just like I've waited for the last few months."

Her mouth dropped open in shock and then she had to know more. "Who's that woman I saw at your house that time?" It was twice, but she didn't want him to know she'd been counting.

"She's someone involved with my work. You don't need to worry about her, or anyone else. I'm a one-woman man." He shook his head. "You'll never need to be concerned about that."

A giggle tumbled from her lips. Any other time, she would've probed more about his work. She had so many questions to ask, but it scared her that he was talking like they were on the border of starting some kind of relationship.

It was nice to be wanted.

"Would you ever consider joining the community?"

At that point, she was certain he'd run away. Instead, he said, "My life's motto is, *never say never.*"

Was there a spark of a chance for them?

This was something she'd never seriously considered. All she could do was stare at him.

"Would you ever leave?" he asked.

"Never," she answered without hesitation.

He chuckled. "Tomorrow then?" he asked.

Happiness bubbled within her to overflowing. "Yes, tomorrow." *And the day after, and the day after that,* she wanted to say, because that's what her heart wanted.

They stood there smiling at one another until she turned and walked away feeling as though she was gliding, flying.

Deep in her heart, she knew she was dancing with danger.

Yet, she'd never felt so alive.

I hope you have enjoyed Book 3, A Simple Kiss.

The next book in the series is:
Book 4
Amish Joy

MORE BY SAMANTHA PRICE

The next book in the series is:

Book 4

Amish Joy

Shocking secrets are revealed when Florence finds out about the English neighbor from next door. Will she feel the same when she learns the truth?

Meanwhile, Florence's stepmother is growing closer to Amish widower, Levi Brunner, and Florence doesn't know how she feels about that. She's certainly not ready for a replacement father.

Her step-sister Joy is still consumed with her feelings for Isaac and is determined to find out exactly how he feels. Joys plans are delayed when Mercy returns with news.

Will Florence risk losing everything, her faith and the apple orchard, for a man who's kept the truth covered for so long? Could a surprise visitor change everything?

Check my website for updates on new releases.

www.SamanthaPriceAuthor.com

ABOUT SAMANTHA PRICE

A prolific author of Amish fiction, Samantha Price wrote stories from a young age, but it wasn't until later in life that she took up writing full time. Formally an artist, she exchanged her paintbrush for the computer and, many best-selling book series later, has never looked back.

Samantha is happiest on her computer lost in the world of her characters.

To date, Samantha has received several All Stars Awards; Harlequin has published her Amish Love Blooms series, and Amazon Studios have produced several of her books in audio.

Samantha is best known for the Ettie Smith Amish Mysteries series and the Expectant Amish Widows series.

Samantha loves to hear from her readers. Connect with her at:

samanthaprice333@gmail.com

www.facebook.com/SamanthaPriceAuthor

Follow Samantha Price on BookBub

Twitter @ AmishRomance

59474874R00119

Made in the USA
Columbia, SC
04 June 2019